Love Just Is

Kate Murray

First published in 2014

by

RAGING AARDVARK PUBLISHING, Brisbane, Australia

Cover Image, Illustrations and Design © by

Kate Murray

ISBN: 0-9875331-6-9
ISBN-13: 978-0-9875331-6-6

For Mum

CONTENTS

ACKNOWLEDGMENTS

With thanks to Elaine, the editor who worked all hours, and to Annie for saying yes. And to everyone who had a word of encouragement when the end seemed too far away, you know who you are and I thank you with all my heart.

Kate Murray

EROS

to the ends of the earth

1 FATE

My granddad used to say that we are the sum of what we endure, and he would have known suffering, as he had polio as a child and experienced pain throughout his life. I was thinking about this on that bleak November morning in the curious half-sleep that visits the anxious, when a terrifying hammering on my front door caused me to sit up sharply, gripped by uncontrollable shaking. The odd thing was that I knew the knock was coming. It had been ten days since they had forced their way into the bedroom and taken Travis ... God, I missed him.

It started simply enough; in fact I barely even registered the news article, the first one. It was a quick one line on the scrolling tape and a few short words, I don't even remember if there had been a picture or footage, just a disembodied voice saying that China appeared to have a small outbreak of some sort of new bird flu. Bird flu! They didn't even get that right. It wasn't bird flu, but by the time they had worked that out we all knew about it.

Travis had come home one day saying that half his work-mates were ill. Instead of increasing the hours of the remaining staff they were going to close the call centre for a while. I didn't believe him at the time, but he insisted, kept on insisting all that night and the next morning. I questioned him right up to the time I watched the small portable TV in the kitchen. I'd been drinking fresh orange at the time. I always had fresh orange in the morning, as it was meant to hold colds at bay. Travis laughed and told me it was a silly idea, especially when we ate so much fruit and veg, but I clung to my superstition. Of course, it does seem to have worked; after all I am still here and Travis is ...

So I was watching the television when Travis came and put his arms around me. Such strong arms, and they'd hold me just right, so I felt safe. I leant back and we watched it together. This anchor-man was on the news and I remember saying, "I thought he was retired?" Travis shrugged; I felt it all along my back. Then he was saying that there was a new flu virus going round, and that if anyone felt ill they were to call the number on the screen and not go to the doctor. It was then that Travis twisted away from me and sneezed; a really big one, and I said bless you and he gave me that look.

He never believed in any of the God stuff either. I mean, neither did I, but some things were traditional, and God bless you was one of them. It's funny now, in a dark way. That saying was first used to bless people with plague and I'd used it for Travis. So funny, can't you hear me laughing? Strange, how it sounds more like crying. That first sneeze was the beginning. Then came the cough and the temperature, and then he got better. But I'd already called the number, and the doctor and his entourage arrived in those plastic yellow suits, their breathing harsh and sounding like villains in a science fiction film. They had scared me with their mechanical, "don't panic" and plastic pats on my arm. The feel of their gloves and the smell of that warm rubber was just nasty. You couldn't get away from it. Because we were quarantined they didn't want us to open the window, I did though, once they were gone. Just a little. I had to. The smell, not only of the suits but of Travis, was too much. To make matters worse it was also one of the hottest summers I can remember.

Like I said though, I was able to ring them about ten days ago and say that it looked like Travis was getting better. Except it didn't work like that, not that I knew at the time. Still, I felt that it was a miracle. After days in bed barely moving, he suddenly sat up, looked around and saw me.

"Hey, baby," he said, smiling, and for a moment I forgot his pallor and the fact that he had lost most of his hair. He was just Travis. "Any chance of a cuppa?"

I tingled all over and said yeah, no problem. I went downstairs to put the kettle on; we still had power then. I called the centre.

"Don't worry," I said, "he's getting better." They just said there would be someone around tomorrow to see if he was still improving and I said that was okay and that he should be fine by then. They said of course and put the phone down. I made the tea and took it to him. I will never forget walking into the room and seeing my man, the person I had pinned all my hopes on, just lying there.

They say hope is hard to kill and I know, because I thought at that time, standing in the stinking room, that he had just lain down to sleep, that he hadn't wanted to get up and shower that gross smell and stale sweat off him. Hope, it's unforgiving. I tip-toed to his bedside. He just lay with his eyes open, not seeing anything. I put a hand on his shoulder and shook him. His head wobbled back and forth like a rag doll's. I don't remember dropping the cup or holding him, but I did wake up at some point and it was dark outside. I reached over to switch the light on, but it didn't work. I was holding him, cradling him to my chest and he was cold, completely cold and stiff. That freaked me out. I jumped out of the bed and the smell hit me. I can't even describe it. I ran to the bathroom and fell over something, I think it was a scrunched up pair of jeans. I fell hard and just lay there for a moment. The smell was less here and I could just make out the flaky scent of dust. They say that dust is mostly skin, dead skin that has just fallen off and been replaced, so in effect I was breathing in my Travis. I cried then; sobbed and wailed at the wrongness of it all.

I must have fallen asleep or passed out, but it was the sun on my face that brought me round. That and the heavy banging on the door. Just like now. Boom, boom. Except that then I scrambled up and ran down the stairs, using the light that filtered through the windows to see through my dusty, ill-used home.

"Where is he?" they asked in their false voices. I just pointed and they stormed upstairs. It seemed like seconds later that they appeared with a body, Travis, in one of those black bags. Then one stopped in front of me. "Did you touch him after he died?"

That voice was freaky, it had no inflection. I couldn't tell if he pitied me or was laughing. His faceplate was just like those you see on spacemen, all gold and reflective. I shrugged. I really didn't care what happened; my reason for living was leaving in a bag and with him were all my dreams; the house, the babies, everything. But the spaceman wouldn't leave. He held my arm and shook me.

"Did you…" he started but I didn't let him finish. Instead I yelled in his face, yes! He took a step back and dropped my arm. Maybe it was because I hadn't drunk anything in a while, at least twelve hours, but I had a coughing fit. They ran out of the house and I heard them close the door. I was alone. For a moment I just stood there and then looked around. It was dusty inside and the sun coming in through the windows made it look like an abandoned house. I felt abandoned so, I reasoned, why not the house? It was morning and I needed some comfort, something. So I went to the kitchen and to the fridge. It smelt bad; the power had been off for a while and a lot of the food was rotten. The orange juice was fine though. Briefly I wondered what sort of preservatives they used to make it last that long. But really it was just a small thought. I poured a pint of juice and downed half of it. Honestly, that was the best thing I'd ever drunk, ever tasted. I found myself in front of the TV, watching the blank screen, wishing for Travis to put his arms around me and his chin on the top of my head, just like he used to; to hold me safe. He didn't. For a moment I actually felt angry with him. How dare he leave me? Right then, at that moment, I decided that I wanted to live, that I would live for us both.

Which is why, when they came for me ten days later, I felt fear. I know why they left it so long. It had taken ten days for Travis to die; damn, it had only taken ten days for the whole world to go to hell in a hand-basket. In that time I had cleaned the house and packed. I hoped that they would see I was fine and then leave, but I'd also heard gunshots lately. I mean, this is a middle-class suburb in England; there would have been no guns unless they were military. I didn't check outside, I didn't even look, just in case there were scavengers. Instead I lived in my bubble, pretending that I was waiting for Travis to come home. True, it had been hard with no power and maybe I'd lost some weight, but at least I had time, just to say goodbye.

The banging increased and then I heard the door go, a sharp crack of a sound. Then silence. I expected to hear the rasps of their breath and see the yellow suits, but nothing. I remembered my Granddad again, and the fact he always said that what we imagine is far worse than it ever is. I am dressed. I walk down the stairs and there, in the front room, is a man.

"Hello?" I call out and he turns. Travis's eyes look at me. I sit, there on the stairs I just collapse into a sitting position.

The man takes step toward me. "Emma?"

I cry. He has Travis's eyes.

"Emma, where is Travis?"

I just shake my head. How can I tell him that his son is dead? It must be something I say or how I look but I see the realisation in his eyes, and then I am engulfed. Travis had been hard and young, his hugs a cage of protection, but his father's are soft and yet comforting. I feel safe.

"Come on," he says, pulling away and leading me to the door. "You are coming with me."

"Where?" I ask.

He smiles and looks down. Travis, as he would have been in twenty years' time. "Home."

I nod. I will go; after all I have no other choice. I don't know why I am still alive but I must live. As we leave I look back and there, on the door, is a white cross. How ironic, I think and the Travis I hold safe in my heart agrees. His father sees me looking.

"They used the same goddamn mark as the 1500's. Stupid bastards. They sealed people up then too. They are even calling it the Black Plague."

I blink up at him. "No," I say, "it isn't the black plague, it is just fate."

He blinks at me and I smile. He shakes his head and takes me to a large Landrover. I jump in, careful not to hit my stomach on the door. Fate has a way of taking everything and, just when you know you can't take it anymore, she gives it back, just a little, just enough to give you hope. I'll have to tell him, but later. Just for the moment this is my secret, this is my fate, and my hope.

2 THE LETTER

Sitting on the upper deck of the bus into town Neil remembered The Plaza, that temple of a cinema near where he grew up. Now it was apartments. He thought about how, in time, even the most solid monuments become snow, and all passed time, a minute. Again he opened that letter of forty years ago and stared at the neat writing. Meredith must have sat and printed out her handwriting, just so he could read it.

Merry had two writing styles, one that looked like a spider had died and the other, well, the other was what he was gazing at. He once asked her why she used both. She had shrugged.

"It's just that sometimes you want to be read."

"So why have the other style?"

"Because sometimes you want to hide," she had said with a smile. He had smiled back but she averted her gaze, as if his face held some secret that she couldn't look at.

"Are you alright?" he'd asked and Merry had reached over and squeezed his hand. At the time he thought it was in reassurance, but now, looking back, it may not have been. How many times had he asked? And how many times had she ignored the question or pointed at something else.

"What shape do you think that cloud is?" Her voice had been bright and cheerful. He had played along, too scared not to. It would have been too hard to have confronted the dull look in her eyes and the dark circles beneath them.

"I think it looks like a dog," he'd said on that day. The day she had written the letter.

"A black dog?"

"No, the cloud is white. The dog can't be black."

"It is," she said. "That dog is black."

"Why?" he'd asked and for the first time Merry looked at him in surprise.

"Because it's my dog."

"You don't own a dog," he said and playfully pushed her shoulder.

She had flinched away from him, acting as if he had tried to hit her. He looked at her then, her too thin frame and wide hurt eyes. Up until that point their relationship had been in the present. She had asked for it that way and he had seen no reason not to follow her lead.

Sitting on the bus he winced at his own recollection. It had been easier to just do as he was told, even though he should have known there was a problem. Instead he had ignored it. She had become more silent and withdrawn.

"But you haven't got a dog," he'd said on that day.

"I have," she said. "We all have, but most don't get to see it." She had looked up at the cloud. "Is it beautiful?"

He had not looked up, but instead gazed at her. "Yes."

"Good, I always wanted it to be beautiful." Then she had risen from the bench they were sitting on. "I'm off home."

He had started to rise, but she placed a hand on his chest, pushing him back down. "You can stay here. I need some time."

He looked from her hand, so tiny and thin that he could count the small bones, just like a bird, and looked at her face. She had smiled sadly and placed a chaste kiss on his lips. Then she had gone, walking away with her white blonde hair blowing in a soft breeze.

Looking at the letter he held in his hand he closed his eyes, imagining that the breeze he felt now was the one she had felt. That they existed at the same time. Except he could not forget that she was not here. She had left him on that bench.

Neil tried to imagine her thoughts, but he couldn't. How had she gone home and sat down to write the letter with no emotion? Or had she cried? One of his nightmares was of her writing the letter and then going to the bathroom and then writing the letter and going through the same time loop, but every time she picked up the pen a new emotion would pass before her; sometimes anger, sometimes fear. Once she laughed and another time she appeared to be forced to write, although there had only been her there to hold the pen straight. In every dream though she would cry out his name and in every one he was unable to reach her. All he could do was watch from behind glass, present but not with her.

He understood that it was their relationship he saw in that letter and the simple fact he had taken and never given back.

On the top of the bus the old man looked up and realised he needed the next stop. Climbing from the top, holding tightly to the rail, he shuffled his way down. No one paid him attention, he was too old and too ordinary.

"Next stop," he rasped and the driver didn't acknowledge him. Neil knew better than to ask again. They could get upset.

When the bus stopped he got off and Merry went with him. But where he had aged she had remained the same. She danced between those on the pavement. Forever with him, but too far away to touch or feel. She was everything around him, a snatch of honey scent on the air, a leaf that brushed his face, and the sound of a sigh that was no more than the wind in the trees. Through his self-imposed torturous journey he walked with his head down, not meeting anyone's eyes.

Finally he came to the white building. There was no one on the pavement as he turned. Walking up the steps he went through an arch into the garden. There he walked to a bank of box shelves in the wall. Each was meticulously labelled. He stopped at one and sat on the bench opposite.

Three rows up and on the tenth column Merry awaited his visit. Forty years was a long time and although they never married he knew that they ought. Taking a small red stone from his pocket he held it in his hand for a moment and then stood. Walking over he pulled open the stone door and placed it inside.

Turning, he walked away, rubbing a worn corner of the letter between his thumb and fingers. Her words reassured him.

"I will be with you always." Pausing he looked up and down the street. At one end a black dog passed and caught his eye. He smiled. She was right, their dog was black.

3 BLUE HERON

The man walked from his car in the driveway, noticing the light was on in the kitchen, but before he could consider who had turned it on he was forced to drop to the ground, flinching as a Heron swooped so low that he had to get out of the way. The cooling shadow of the bird passed and he turned onto his back, watching the stars as they blinked in and out while invisible clouds passed in the night. The hangover he had been nursing all day had developed into a migraine and now it appeared he was being burgled. Perhaps if Lisa had been here, he wouldn't be lying on his back on the path hoping his life would blink out like the stars above him. But she was gone, taken by some celestial hand that, according to her damn parents, was kindly. He didn't think so. No one should have to go through that agony. Tom smacked his head against the paving stone under him, welcoming the pain. Pain was a distraction and, as Johnny Cash said, it showed he was still alive. Well, in that case he really was.

Tom knew he wasn't doing great since Lisa went, leaving long before she had passed, her skeletal figure bundled into blankets and wheeled out to a waiting ambulance. But then his life had meaning. He had woken every morning and his sole purpose had been to get to hospital and hold her hand. She had always maintained that he would leave. She would place a tiny hand on his chest and push him away.

"You will leave me," she would say without any emotion. "They all do."

He would kiss her palm. "Never." And he meant it. She had been his life. And now that she was gone he had no life. Looking up he watched the light go out in his kitchen. At least they were leaving.

Tom awoke to a hand shaking him.

"You can't stay here."

Tom looked up. "Someone's in my house," he slurred.

The voice continued. "You did used to live here…, but you sold it."

Tom sat up and wondered at the spinning world. "I saw a heron."

"Yes," the voice said, "it's your choice of drink, blue heron." There was a clatter as a bottle spun toward him. Blearily he saw the heron on the label, as he became aware of a bad smell, of cloying sweat and alcohol. If Lisa could see him now she would be so disappointed. She would lean forward so he could smell her cinnamon scent under the medication and say, "I told you that you would leave me." Then he would feel her warm tears fall onto him, chilling him to his very core.

LUDUS

play games, all sorts

4 THE WEDDING

Mrs Rosen sniffed uninterestedly at the cucumber sticks. "Why do you think they do it?"

"Do what?" Her companion asked, eyes never settling on one person or group but, like some extinct butterfly that flitted from plant to plant, darted from face to face. In her head she counted off those that ought to be there and those that weren't. She also made note of the packages.

"Mrs Jones, I do believe that you aren't listening!"

"What?" Mrs Jones turned her wide stare to her friend. "I am. It's just that the Martins are over there. Look at the size of their present!"

Mrs Rosen turned her piggy eyes to the family in question, wrinkling her nose at the children who never seemed to be clean. The family of four held a small prize, a small square box wrapped in… "Is that newspaper?"

"Yes, they are new age or some such nonsense."

Mrs Rosen shook her head, her many chins and jowls shaking with the movement.

Behind her, and unseen by either woman, a group of children copied Mrs Rosen, making their arms rounded away from their bodies copying her rotund figure. One girl, the same girl that Mrs Jones had once scared into a screaming fit just by smiling at her, went on tip toe and tried to appear thin and gaunt, reflecting Mrs Jones. Although the children did a basic job of the impersonations a mother spied her son walking like an elephant behind Mrs Rosen and called him into line. The two women heard her and both turned their vulture eyes on the children who parted and ran. They knew that although Mrs Rosen appeared cuddly she was likely to clip you around the ear. Mrs Jones, all sharp angles and points, would yell at you but that was it. Most thought that it was because she was so skinny a five year old could knock her over.

Of course Mrs Rosen wished to have a figure like Mrs Jones whilst Mrs Jones wanted to be less skinny. It was almost as if their friendship was only designed to show them what they wanted, each staring at the other with envy and a little anger. In the ten years they had been friends neither woman had changed her body shape or countenance. If anything they had settled more securely into their roles. Locally known as the hedge-peerers they would know what was happening before anyone else. Mrs Jones had a small dog, some sort of terrier crossed with a whippet. It was a beautiful little dog, and she took it everywhere. At first everyone had wondered at her devotion but it soon became apparent that Mrs Jones used her dog to listen in. An argument at number ten? Mrs Jones is walking past with her little dog, giving the skinny creature all the exercise it needs. In fact, half the village were worried that the poor little dog would wear down its legs.

The wedding was between the eldest child of the Martins who, in Mrs Jones opinion, had wonderful taste in curtains but not in carpets, and the youngest son of the Ball clan. Those annoying Ball children. Perhaps the youngest was the best, but still, no middle-class family had any right to birth five. Mrs Rosen sniffed in disdain as the groom passed close with all four of his siblings. She had no idea what the family had been thinking, after all, the only thing they seemed to have done was put their limited financial resources under stress.

Shaun passed the pair, their glasses full of champagne and yet both looked like they had taken a sip of lemon juice. He frowned, certain that he hadn't invited them. Yet there they were, Mrs Rosen staring at him and Mrs Jones turning a dour gaze upon Karin. Looking at her his heart swelled, still not certain why she had married him. He had definitely got the better deal and he was not going to allow a couple of old biddies to ruin the day.

"Karin?"

The bride turned with a radiant smile on her face. She was mid-laugh so she just raised her eyebrows, silently asking what was wrong.

"Did you invite the gruesome twins?" Shaun asked.

Karin looked behind him and frowned. "No, I never liked them. Hold up, Mum did the list."

Karin turned and walked to the head table, where a happy but exhausted mother of the bride sat, decked out in magenta and black.

"Mum? Did you invite the horror twins?"

Looking behind her daughter Maud was about to say no, when her eye was caught by Philip, her nephew. "Oh my god!"

Karin swung around and looked behind her. First she noted the two battle-axes staring at her and then she saw Philip. "Oh, he never has."

Shaun looked on with a smile on his face. Karin thumped his shoulder. "What are we going to do?" she asked.

"Nothing."

"Why?"

"Because your wonderful cousin is going to take care of our little problem." And sure enough as they watched they saw Philip clock the pair and start toward them.

"Should we stop him?" Maud asked.

"No," said Shaun. "This should be entertaining."

Across from them Mrs Rosen and Mrs Jones watched the exchange.

"What do you think has got them worried?" Mrs Rosen asked.

"I don't know. The poor quality of the champagne?" answered Mrs Jones.

"It does taste like dishwater."

"Horrible."

"Disgusting."

Both looked down at their glasses as if they held oozing slime instead of champagne.

"Ladies," a voice said. Both looked up and into Philip's face. Both sniffed in recognition.

"I would like to introduce my date. This is Crystal and this is Rose." Philip laughed, his rich baritone lending a musical note to the outburst. "Maybe that ought to be dates."

On either arm a blonde twin giggled uncontrollably. He gave an indulgent smile. "Ladies, this is Mrs Rosen and Mrs Jones."

The girls smiled and held out limp-wristed hands to the older women.

Mrs Rosen stared at the hand in front of her in horror, her face slowly turning from red to a vivid beetroot colour.

"Nice to meet you," the woman in front of her said. "I'm Crytal."

"I'm sure you are," Mrs Rosen said in an explosion of sound.

Crystal raised an eyebrow and let her hand drop.

Mrs Jones just stared at Rose. "But... But... There are two of you."

Rose dropped her hand. "Yes, we are identical twins."

Mrs Rosen sniffed and turned away. Mrs Jones followed suit and they walked over to the waiter holding a tray of champagn. They started to place theirs, but were stopped.

"If you could hand those to the waitress," the man said.

Both women sneered and looked around them. Near the exit there was a waitress, just standing and talking to a guest. Mrs Rosen and Mrs Jones set off at quick trot. Neither woman noticed the gazes from the other guests as they transversed the hall. Reaching the waitress they slammed their glasses onto the tray.

"I wouldn't stay..." started Mrs Rosen.

"...here another minute," finished Mrs Jones. And with that they were gone, leaving the faint smell of lavender and rose water.

Philip walked to the middle of the hall with his twins and bowed. Spontaneous applause erupted.

Outside the two women paused as the noise roared out of the hall.

"What do you think that's about?" Mrs Rosen asked.

"Maybe someone fell?" Mrs Jones replied.

Laughing they walked away, pleased that they had made their escape before the cake had been cut.

5 SEARCHING PRIDE

Justin sat in the black leather chair and slowly turned one way and the other in a strangely graceful motion. The repetitive movement calmed him but every pass of the chair highlighted the piece of bright white paper with insults scrawled over it on the desk. With every turn he saw that sheet and his tension rose, radiating out of his shoulders and passing down his back. He had no choice though; the fiasco with Laura had left him alone. Perhaps if she hadn't come home early and caught him... Best not to think about it. He moved faster as he tried to rid himself of the feelings of shame and guilt. He hadn't asked for these obsessions, they just happened and the only way to reduce them was with alcohol and he had no wish to pass the next six months in a daze.

Pushing back from the desk he rose and stalked away from the chair. The violent movement made him feel better, as did the pacing as he appeared to wear a path in the small office carpet. It was ironic really that he was alone, after all, with his good looks he ought to have girls lining up, but instead Laura had put the fear of God into him. He stopped and stretched, enjoying the feeling of silk as it shifted across his muscles; he worked out and most people described him as a Jude Law in looks but with the body of a surfer. In school he hadn't been tall, hell, he still wasn't now, so he had made sure his body was fit, trying to make himself the opposite of a victim. He knew he was handsome and had made himself the epitome of male desirability. As he entered a room he was aware that all eyes would turn to him and remain on him. He was always surprised how many of those eyes were male, not that he minded, he liked attention and a brief warning soon made any admirers realise he was firmly heterosexual. He took pride in his physique, in his broad shoulders and narrow waist, but perhaps what was most striking was his hair. It fell to his waist in a shaggy cut that could only be described as mane-like and its' colour was old gold.

Justin was an unusual man with enough magnetism to hold a roomful of attention and keep it with his self assured movements and grace. Laura had once described him, before the incident, as a man who was totally comfortable in his own skin. It gave him an attractiveness that was addictive.

Except that his sexual preferences were somewhat different to those of others. With Laura he had tried to hide and give her what he knew she wanted. He had gone against his polygamous nature and given his all to nurturing the relationship Laura needed. He had hoped that after she had seen his true proclivity and run out of the house she would just disappear. But what was the old adage? Never date someone at work? He understood that now. The rumours and sneers had become so bad that he had to take up the situation with his boss, Miss Rebecca Cob.

He walked into her office and sat in the rather awkward seat. Automatically he made himself comfortable by stretching his legs and throwing an arm over the back of the chair. Rebecca watched him with a slight smile on her face. Once he was settled, she got up, walked around him and locked the door. He scowled, not sure how this meeting was going to unfold.

"I've heard the rumours," she said, walking back to her chair.

Justin's face became expressionless as he tried to appear nonchalant. "I don't know what to do... I can always leave." Weariness stole over him and he realised that he would, despite loving his job. He just wanted to be left alone.

"Under no circumstances will you be leaving," she stated calmly. "This treatment is tantamount to bullying, so Laura will be reprimanded." She glanced at his shocked face, squinting over her glasses. "Is it true?"

Justin froze. For a second he had thought it would be fine, that he could stay...

"Justin," Rebecca said with a smile, "are you a furry?"

He blinked for a moment, his composure gone. She had used the colloquial term and not 'zoophile'. He knew that this could be a mistake and he was putting his career on the line but he nodded, not completely trusting his voice.

"Good," she said, sitting back in her seat with a smile.

He leaned slightly forward, anxious and surprised. "Are you?" His voice sounded rough and too low.

"Oh yes."

Justin couldn't believe it. Rebecca! He hadn't seen that coming. He'd moved here over a year ago and thought he was the only one in the area. "Yip?"

Rebecca didn't answer but gave him a knowing smile. Justin sighed with relief. She was furry and a yip, which meant there had to be a group, a sexually active one at that.. He could find people he wouldn't have to hid his true nature from.

"Looking at you I would have thought you're a Leo."

"It's the hair? Right?" he said, amused.

Rebecca nodded. "That, and the fact you are probably the strongest alpha I've seen in ages."

Justin leant back and felt himself relax. "Yourself?"

"Lets just say my last name has not always been Cob."

That was all he needed to know. She was a horse in her alter ego and unfortunately a prey animal for a lion, not a potential mate.

"Are you coming to the convention?" It had been an innocent question from Rebecca but had opened a huge new world.

Now Justin sat in front of a piece of paper trying to put together an advert so that he could find a mate, or rather a pride. Finally he stopped pacing and walked over to the desk. Moving the chair out of the way and leaning over he wrote just six words:

Six tails wanted for sexual pride.

STORGE

blood is thicker than water

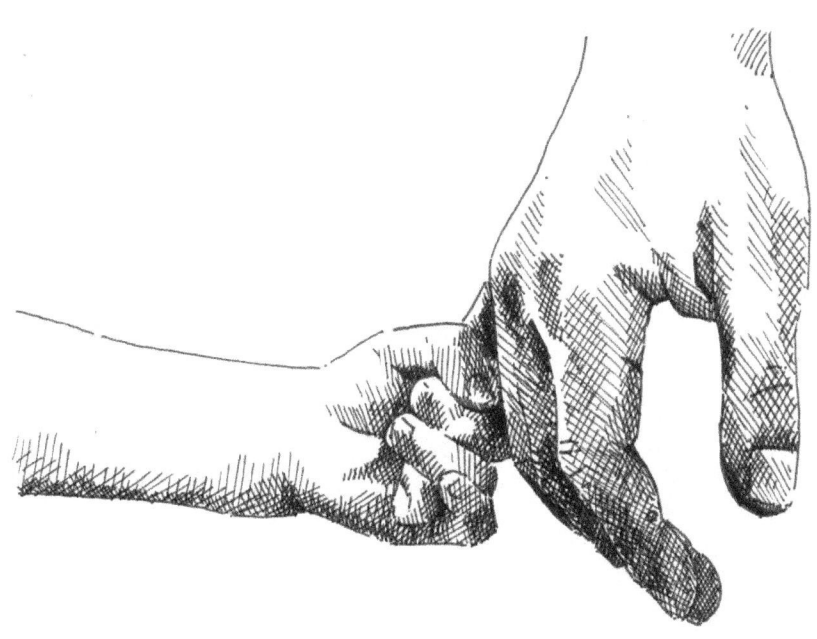

6 THE RUN

Nelson's Row is the toughest street in Clapham. Hell, even the coppers go down it in twos; too scared to take the walk alone. So it is surprising when a small boy of about fifteen turns into the street with a swagger in his step and a smile on his face. The street is quiet, but then it is about four thirty in the morning and most of the houses won't begin to show life for another half an hour. The lad goes to one side of the street, leans against the wall and lights a cigarette. Taking an empty packet from his trouser pocket he carefully opens it out so it is a flat piece of cardboard. He then carefully folds the pack back up leaving the rough card on the outside. The gold insert that is still stuck to the bottom he carefully rips off and drops. The small piece of paper blows away and floats onto a step just down from where the boy is standing.

"Oi! Tom! This yours?"

Tom looks over and blushes. "Sorry, missus," he says and walks over. "He in?"

The woman looks at him and places her hands on her hips. "He is," she says, glaring at the boy. She doesn't want to see him, not with him wanting money, but doesn't want to say anything, not with her husband inside and within earshot. Stepping aside she says, "Go in and mind the bucket."

Tom nods and ducks inside, turning as he passes her to place a quick peck on her cheek. He has to go up on tiptoe but her blush and smile is worth it.

"Cheeky sod," she says and pushes him in the direction of the sitting room. As he turns to enter she taps her head and Tom dutifully removes his flat cap. Inside, the range is burning and giving off a welcome heat. In the one good chair sits a large man.

"Let's hear them," he says with a gruff voice. Tom gets out the cigarette pack and a small stub of pencil. The man doesn't even look up; instead he lists off a series of names and numbers. When he stops he finally hands the boy a small envelope of cash. Tom finishes writing down the figures and takes the cash. "You got all that?"

"Yes, sir."

He turns back to the range and Tom knows he is dismissed. Popping the pack and the cash in his pocket he heads to the front door. The Missus is on her hands and knees scrubbing the step. Tom can see her hair is just turning grey and her hands are chapped raw from the water. For a moment he stands quiet, then he says, "Missus, I need to get out."

The woman looks at her clean step and sighs. Standing she lets him pass. Tom takes a step back and launches into the air, missing the step and landing in the cobbled street, his metal bottomed boots ringing sparks into the road. The woman ruffles his hair, a smile on her face.

"Go on with you, Tom." He grins and jogs off, his boots clattering his progress.

The next three houses run without a hitch and Tom knows he only has one more to do. He's left this one to last. The Missus of this house is young and Tom likes her. Her old man he doesn't know. He works and Tom doesn't see him. Instead she will give him the bets. As he walks to the house he sees that she is scrubbing the step, later than the others. Stopping next to the step he coughs.

"Tom," she says warmly. "You okay?"

Tom grins. "Yes, missis, fine. Yourself?"

She ignores the fact that he has asked only about herself and not her husband. "We are both fine, thank you, Tom. How's your mam?"

"She's good." Tom reaches into his pocket to bring out the packet.

"Not today, Tom. Said this morning he didn't feel lucky." She grins. "Try tomorrow."

"Okay," Tom says with a sigh. Not having a bet from them would cut his money, but it couldn't be helped. "See you tomorrow."

He turns to leave. Just as he does two coppers start along the street. "Tom!" The woman behind him calls. Standing, she picks up her bucket and walks inside, motioning him to follow. Not needing to be asked twice he steps into the terrace behind her. "Go into the living room." He does and she closes the door just as the coppers come into view.

"They're probably going to be knocking on doors in a bit," Tom says. The woman nods and goes to the range. There, on top, are some warming rolls. She grabs one and shoves it into his hand.

"The back door." She points past the scullery.

Tom leans forward and pecks her cheek, turns, and is gone. She sighs and wonders why she is willing to risk trouble for Tom, a bookie's runner. Then the answer comes to her. She sees him almost every day and he has become family. Hell, he's become family for the whole street. She's doing no more than anyone else would. A knock sounds at the door and she jumps. Sighing, she walks to the front and opens the door. She says nothing.

"You seen the kid?" one says.

She remains silent. Behind her she faintly hears Tom's boots scrape the top of the wall and she smiles at the coppers.

7 THE LAST REQUEST

Dan stood at the bar.

"Well, boy, this is it. Here endeth life's lesson and beginneth the journey to the long box and eternal fire."

"Jesus Christ," said Tom. "What are you talking about?"

"I've got a tumour. They've given me three weeks to live. Drinks all round."

Silence descended as Tom and the bargirl, May, looked at Dan. It was a slow night and there were only the two patrons in the Lamb's Fleece.

"You're kidding?" Tom said, eyes wide and mouth open.

"No," Dan said sadly.

The girl averted her eyes and poured the tramp a drink.

"Is there nothing they can do?" Tom asked, accepting the pint.

"No. Too advanced and too many places. Said it started in my prostate but has now taken root in the pancreas."

"Does it hurt?" May asked tentatively as she handed over a pint and whiskey chaser. Dan shook his head and reached for his wallet. May enclosed his large strong hand with hers. "It's on the house," she said quietly. Dan nodded and, for a moment, hung his head, letting out a huge sigh. Next to him Tom looked at his pint and in two swallows destroyed half of it. He wasn't quite sure what to do if Dan cried. Can you hug a man you hardly know? True, he had sat next to him for the last year if not more, but he didn't even know where he lived. He dressed posh, in a suit and even a tie, and always had money. At first Tom had ignored him and got on with forgetting his own life, but after a while he'd started to warm to the guy. He never preached and always had a full wallet.

"Funny thing is," Dan said, straightening and looking at May, "I'm only here for work."

A puzzled expression filled both Tom and May's faces. "Work?" May asked, suddenly aware she was still covering Dan's hand with her own. Quickly she removed it and started cleaning the counter, trying to hide her embarrassment. Although she was closer to Tom's age, Dan's self-assurance and kind eyes had always drawn her to him. Of course he'd never shown any sign of being interested, who would? May knew she was 'the girl next door', with mousey hair, brown eyes and nondescript features. She wasn't ugly but pretty in a forgettable way. May had always known there was no hope for them but still she had dreamed and now even the dream was going to be taken away.

A slight smile played across Dan's lips. "Yeah, work."

"What do you do?" May asked cleaning a spill.

"I'm a PI."

Next to him Tom froze and stiffened. May didn't notice.

"You're working on a case?"

"Yep. Cracked it last week. Diagnosed this week. Talk about bipolar news." Dan let out a laugh that contained no humour at all and May winced at his bark.

"Anyone we know?" Dan raised an eyebrow asking a silent question.

She explained, "Well, in the movies all the PI's are looking for someone. Unless they are taking photos of affairs and there isn't any of those here." May sighed as if a bit of scandal would make her day, which it probably would.

"I am looking for someone. Found them a year ago. A runaway. And it's taken me this long to confirm their identity."

Tom just stared into his pint, trying to make himself as small as possible.

"A runaway," May whispered. "Do you know why?"

Dan nodded. "The family explained it all. Turned out their son was a bit of a handful so they decided to send him into the military. He refused and instead decided to enrol into Art College. From what I've seen he was quite talented. Painted portraits. Anyway the family locked him up so he ran."

"Locked him up?" May asked. "This is the twenty first century. People don't get locked up." She had stopped cleaning and was leaning on the bar giving Dan her full attention.

"They did. Locked him in his room. Refused to let him out until he willingly enrolled in the military."

"And?"

"After two months he ran."

"Wow! And you found him?"

Dan nodded.

"What do you do now?"

"Well, normally I'd contact the family and let them handle it, but I know the man and I like him so I'm going to leave it up to him."

"Who...?" May started but Tom interrupted.

"I'm not going back," he said in a quiet voice.

May looked at him, shocked. When Tom had first started coming into the bar, perhaps a few years ago, she'd thought him a catch; broad shoulders, blonde hair and blue eyes, and when he smiled he had a roguish look that suited him and left her weak at the knees. Of course that was two years ago and two years of heavy drinking could do a lot to a man. His shoulder-length hair was lank and unwashed. He smelt like a drunk. His clothes were always stained and his eyes just appeared dead. The sparkle she had seen in the beginning had been washed away by the amount of alcohol he'd drunk.

"I won't go back," Tom said finishing his pint.

Dan smiled and turned to him. He placed a hand on Tom's grimy sweatshirt stopping him from leaving. "Think of it as a dying man's last request?"

"To go back?" Sneered Tom.

"No," Dan said with a sad smile, "to decide to live. You can do what you want. I've told your parents I can't find you. I can't live, the decision has been made for me, but you can. So, my dying request is that you live." Dan paused and his grip tightened. "And I don't mean surviving or slowly killing yourself with this shit." He gestured to the pumps. "Live!"

Tom shook himself free and backed away. "You said you can't find me?"

"That's right, Joseph. I told them you were not in Cornwall."

Tom nodded and turned to leave. As he was about to step through the door he turned. "You really dying?"

Dan gave a sad smile and lifted the pint of beer in salute.

Tom nodded. "I'll see what I can do." And then he gave the smile from two years ago and for a moment his eyes shone. Then he was gone, the door banging behind him and gloom returning to the pub.

Automatically May got out an air freshener and sprayed Tom's seat. The fake chemical smell of a fresh breeze filled the place and drowned out the odour of stale alcohol.

"You really are dying," she stated.

Dan nodded. "Yep."

May nodded, copying him. "I get off at five. You fancy waiting?"

Dan grinned. "Love to. After all what else am I going to do for the next three hours?"

May leaned forward and placed a chaste kiss on Dan's lips, tasting whiskey and beer. They broke apart as the door opened and a gang of students walked in.

"Hey, darling," one called out, giving her a leer, only to stop midway as Dan turned a frosty gaze on him. "Sorry, man. Didn't know she was taken."

Dan just turned away and watched as May served the group. Today was definitely looking up. He smiled into his beer.

8 THE JEWELLED MACKEREL

She sits on the ground watching ants crawl along the wall. The child is mesmerised by the grey blue slate of the dry stones compared to the dull grey of the tarmac. Every now and then a small black ant will crawl up the wall. The girl doesn't know where the ant is going; just that it wants to get there. With a small stick she knocks the ant off just before it reaches the top. The game she has invented is keeping her occupied. She ignores the building crowd behind her and she doesn't think to check for her Mum and Grandparents. She knows she is safe and doesn't think to see if she is missed. Instead she plays her game with her ant, an ant she has christened Toby.

On the other side of the wall the mother and grandparents are lining up to view the spectacle that is about to unfold. "Mum," the daughter turns and passes an anxious glance around her, "you see Crystal?"

Her mother turns and looks about her. "No," she says with a worried expression on her face.

Together the two leave their place in the crowd and start searching. The grandmother stops a young couple. "Have you seen a girl about so high," she indicates just above her knee. "She has blonde hair and is wearing a pink long-sleeve dress?" They look at her for a minute and then both shake their heads and move off. The grandmother shrugs helplessly at her daughter and goes to ask the next person, getting the same response. The mother begins to feel panic grip her and she turns in a slow circle looking for any sign of Crystal. Nothing. "Crystal," she yells, startling an elderly couple near her. "Have you seen her?" she asks.

The couple look at her and the well-dressed man asks, "What

does she look like?"

With relief the mother says, "A girl of about six, blonde, in a pink dress."

"How long has she been missing?"

"I..." she stammers, "I'm not certain. She was playing around and then...," she looks for her mother for help, "she was gone."

The sentence hangs in the air for a moment and then the man looks at his wife. "Did you see anything?"

"There was a little girl playing near the wall," she says with a smile.

"Thank you." The mother moves along the back of the crowd until she is near the sea wall. Checking both sides they can't see her but they do find a name scratched into the dirt – 'Crystal'.

Only a few feet away Crystal wanders away toward where they had parked the car. She hears her mother but is busy having fun dodging between legs; lots of people with trousers and some in leggings. There, someone with a skirt and striped tights. She giggles and twists and turns, skipping and dancing between the people. Her mum's voice gets quieter and quieter but Crystal doesn't notice and, at the moment, doesn't care.

She is skipping and twirling and isn't looking where she is going until a hand lands on her shoulder. "Who are you then?" a gruff voice asks.

Crystal freezes and turns scared eyes up to the man. He is dressed in black with a top hat and although he is smiling she is frightened. Slowly her face crumbles and tears fall from her eyes. "Mum," she wails and, although the crowd parts, no one steps forward. The man looks at the crying child and kneels before her.

"Come now, there's no need to cry," he says. "Have you lost your mum?"

Crystal eyes him through her tears and now he is shorter he doesn't seem that scary and she nods, hiding behind her hands. The man calls over his shoulder and a lady comes up. She is in black as well but she has a kind face.

"What do we have here?" she asks.

"Well, I caught a little girl," the man says with a smile, "and I think she has lost her mum."

"Oh, no," the woman says looking around. Then, placing a hand on the man, she gets him to move and takes his place. This lady isn't scary at all and Crystal has stopped crying and is just peeping through her fingers curiously. "What's your name, bach?" the lady asks.

Crystal shyly lowers her hands and gives a hesitant smile, "Crystal."

"Oh! Crystal. That is a lovely name!" she says, smiling. "Now where did you last see your mum?"

Crystal's bottom lip quivers at the mention of her mum but she points behind her.

"When was that?"

She shrugs her tiny shoulders.

"Okay, bach, let me have a word with the others." The lady stands and turns, walking a little distance away. Crystal waits a moment and then follows. "This little girl is called Crystal and she has lost her mum." About ten people wave at Crystal and she smiles and hides behind the woman. "I thought we could use a little helper and if her mum sees her she can run along."

"Sounds good," one of the men says. All the others nod.

Crystal finds the people odd, but now she is used to the hats she finds it funny that all the men wear them. All the ladies are in black too but Crystal isn't worried. In fact, she slips a grimy hand into the woman's who had been talking to her.

The woman looks down. "Okay, Bach, we are going to be in a sort of play. You see this fish," she points at a huge fish leaning on the side of the road, "well, the men carry it to the sea front and we have to follow and cry."

"Why?"

"Well, we are mourning the loss of the mackerel. But we don't really cry, we just pretend. Do you think you can do that?"

Crystal grins and says she can.

The lady looks down. "No smiling then."

Crystal tries to look sad but can't. A moment ago she had been unable to stop crying and now all she can do is smile.

"Rhiannon," another woman says coming forward, "here's my spare shawl for her."

"Thanks." The lady puts a black shawl around Crystal's shoulders and pulls it up over her hair. Crystal feels the shawl and loves the softness. She put her little hands through the holes and the shawl appears to become like a pair of gloves. Enchanted, she plays with the tassels and wool.

"You lot of mourners ready?" One of the men asks. They all nod and the men bend, placing the fish on their shoulders. They move out first and then the women follow, all wailing and crying out. Behind, Rhiannon and Crystal hold back slightly.

"Remember to look for your mum." Then Rhiannon starts to cry, not as loudly as the others as she keeps an eye out for a distraught mother.

They have only gone about a hundred yards when a frantic, "Crystal!" reaches their ears. Flying out of the crowd the frantic mother and grandmother move toward the child with arms outstretched. Rhiannon stops and bends to the little girl.

"Is that your mum?"

"Yes."

"Okay, off you go then." Crystal takes off and then turns, trying to take the shawl off.

"Don't worry, Bach, you keep it." Rhiannon says with a wave, watching to see Crystal safe into her mother's arms and then turning to catch up with the other mourners.

9 BLACK RUINS

They arrived at Oradour at about two o'clock on a June afternoon. They parked the car and saw the ruins across the road.

"There it is. They left it just as it was when the Germans had finished. So no one would forget," Johnny said.

"We weren't even born," Maggie commented.

"Let's go and look."

"I don't know," Maggie said, rubbing her arms as if caught in a cold breeze. "It feels wrong."

Johnny turned to her. She had shrunk into herself and become almost hunched. She didn't meet his eyes. Holding out his hand he dropped his voice to a smooth tone and, as if speaking to a frightened horse, tried to coax her toward the frontage that had once been a church.

"Come on, Maggie. I really want to see this."

"Why? I don't understand."

"It's history," he said and tried a smile, although Maggie didn't see it as she had yet to look up from the gravelled road.

"It's a history I'd prefer to forget."

Johnny dropped his hand. "Okay, stay here." He turned and started to walk away and then turned back. "It's one thing we can't forget. If we do, it might happen again." Then without another word he left.

Maggie listened to the crunch of his footsteps disappear as he walked into the ruins, pausing briefly to look at the burnt out car in front of the church. When she could no longer hear him Maggie raised her head and pushed her hair out of her eyes. He was gone. Instead she found herself alone, she could hear nothing.

Not even the birds were singing. On the air there seemed the scent of burning. Surely that wouldn't still be detected? But there it was, thick and cloying, rising from the ground around her. In fact, it smelt like fresh smoke.

Looking up she could see smoke in the sky, marring the blue of the perfect day. She gingerly got out of the car, trying to see where the smoke was coming from. Then, as if it were no more than a cloud, it was gone. For a moment she stood, then, still watching the sky, she took a step forward.

"Johnny?" she called into the day, but there was no reply. Of course her voice was too quiet. "Johnny!"

Still nothing. She would have to go and look for him. If he didn't see the fire then he could easily walk into the smoke and he was still recovering from a bad chest cold. At least, that's what she told herself. It had nothing to do with the emptiness of the town that no longer existed. What had the brochure said? One woman and six men had survived from six hundred and forty two men, women and children. Shuddering, she stepped further from the car.

Behind her a footstep sounded on the gravel.

Turning, she looked, but there was nothing.

"Hello," she called in a small voice. No one answered. Maggie backed up a few steps. Still there was no sign of anyone. "I can hear you." Her voice was small and she crossed her hands in front of herself, trying to create a barrier against the unknown. Still there was nothing.

Backing up a little more Maggie's back hit something. She froze. In her mind's eye she tried to remember what was behind her. But all she saw was the empty square with the burnt ruin and the old German car out front. She ought not to have hit anything.

Reaching out a hand she touched something cold, and smooth. Maggie could feel her legs shaking. Turning slowly she found herself touching a car. It did have the same shape as the abandoned wreck, but this one was new. It gleamed in the sun.

What held her gaze was the man behind the wheel. He was old, with white hair and he looked shocked.

"Mlle, sortir de la voie. J'ai failli te frapper!"

"What?" Maggie said.

The man stopped talking and looked around. Maggie did the same and gasped in shock. The square was back as it would have been before the massacre. Turning slowly she saw the buildings and the church, and the people. There were people going about their everyday business.

"Mlle, you are Anglais?"

She turned back and found that the old man had got out of his car and was standing in front of her.

"Yes," she said, and then put a hand to her mouth. If she really was to believe her eyes then she was in occupied France.

The man was looking scared now. People had begun to stop. Three people cycled into the square. Maggie's eyes landed on them and she realised that this must be the 10th of June 1944. The three men cycling would be killed. Slowly she faced the road where the Germans would drive. But there was nothing there, just a blank stretch of gravel and mud. Maybe she was wrong?

"What day is it?" she said.

Behind her the old man reached a hand out. "Come, you must hide."

Maggie pulled out of his grasp. "What day is it?" she repeated louder.

"June the tenth," he said. "Now come, you must hide."

Maggie took a step away from him. "1944?"

"Oui."

"You must hide," she said.

"Oui," the old man said. "Come and hide."

"No, not me," Maggie said, although she did wonder if she ought. "You must hide. The Germans are coming."

The old man looked toward the road. The people gathered around shifted at her words. Some seemed not to be worried whilst others stared to move away from her.

"You have brought them here," one woman said, her bag clutched to her chest.

"No," Maggie said. "They were going to come." Taking a step forward she grabbed hold of the woman's arm, who flinched away from her. Maggie noticed that she was dressed in black and briefly she wondered why. Giving the woman's arm a shake she leaned forward. "Don't go into the church."

The French woman pulled free and started to back away.

"Sorcière," she spat.

Maggie dropped her hand. Everyone was moving away from her, but in the distance she could hear cars, a lot of them. Turning to the road she ignored the retreating steps of the people around her. "It's too late. They are here."

"Who's here?" a male voice asked behind her.

Maggie turned but she already knew who it was. "Where did you go?" she asked in a small voice.

"Just behind the church."

"But I called…"

"I'm sorry, I didn't hear you," Johnny said, noticing that Maggie was very pale. "Are you okay?"

"No," Maggie said, hugging her arms around herself. "I think I saw a ghost."

"Really?" Johnny said, leading her back to the car.

Maggie looked behind them. The square was back to what it had been. The burnt out church stood abandoned and in front the car, only now its ancient curves were covered in rust and the tyre rims stood empty in the company of weeds.

"It was different," she said.

"What was?"

"The square."

"Of course it was." Johnny led her to the car and opened the door. As Maggie got in she heard a sharp sound, like a gunshot.

"Was that a gun?"

"No," Johnny said. "It was a building collapsing."

But as he moved around the car he made sure he did it fast. Maggie unwound her window and looked back at the village. As she did the smell of burning filtered into the car. Johnny sniffed and then sneezed.

"Perhaps we ought to get out of here," he said starting the car and pulling away from the ruins, a town of ghosts.

MANIA

to hold forever

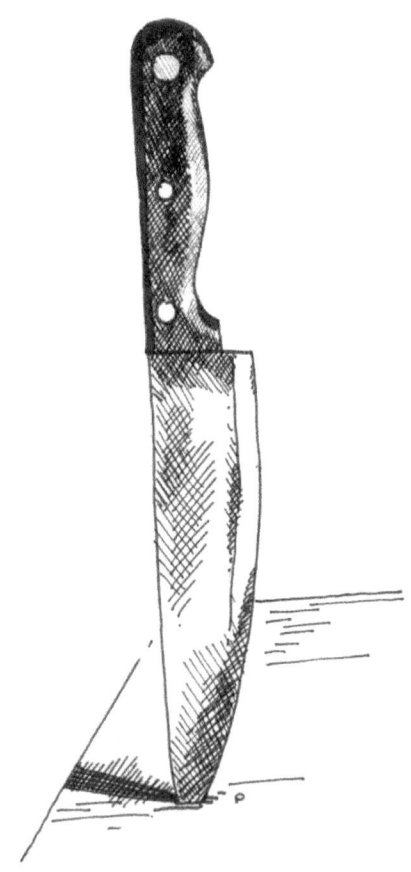

10 LITTLE BOXES

It started with flashing lights speeding around the corner and into my street. I watched them and stood perfectly still. I wasn't trying to hide, it had just been serendipitous. I'd been shopping, run out of milk, again, and as the police had screamed around the corner announcing their presence I leant back into the uncut hedge next to me, hugging the shadows. If they were going for subtle then the police had got it completely wrong. My first thought was, oh shit. And then my second was to shake myself.

I never left a clue, not once, so the only logical explanation had to be that it was about someone else... But there was a nagging doubt. So, instead of stepping out of the shadows and blithely walking down the road, I stayed where I was. In fact, I realised I was outside the abandoned house. Technically it was on the market, but being only a four-roomed terrace I didn't suppose it would ever get sold. So, I slipped into the garden and down the arched alleyway. From here I had access to four gardens that backed onto this, including my own, but what I wanted to do was sit near number four. You see, number four and number six were gossips, they couldn't help it, but their gardens backed onto each other. If I was quiet they would tell me all about it. So I sat on an upturned bucket and opened the chocolate bar I'd bought.

Sure enough, as I am finishing, the two older ladies come out, both quietly walking to the fence.

"Judy?" that is Karen whispering from number four.

"I'm here."

"What's going on?"

"Well, you know Martin? From down the road?"

"Odd boy," Karen said, and I couldn't help but snarl silently. What did she know?

"Yes." I can hear the impatience in Judy's voice and I think that she doesn't really care who it was about, only what the juicy details were.

"Well, according to Bob, he has been killing people."

"Killing?"

I don't wait for any more. That's all I need to know. My cover is blown, again. I wonder where I went wrong this time. It bothers me, but I crawled away from that corner and back to the covered alley. Once there I take out my key. The house?

Well, I don't own it, but it was just standing there empty and I thought it would make a beautiful bolt hole. I'd been right. Of course I hadn't known at the time I was going to need it as I was walking past, but then the gods have always looked favourably at me.

Opening the door I walk in and close it quietly behind me. In the distance I can still hear the ohs and ahs of the two women discussing my habits. For a moment anger lances through me and I growl. I hate people talking about my business and my collection is definitely my business. I suppose the police will dig up my back garden and pull down the new conservatory. They don't have to, I don't keep trophies. Goodness no. Those who do can't move fast. They have to take their 'things' with them. I am free of that. My trophies are in my mind. Take the last.

She'd been walking home. It hadn't been her size or appearance but as I'd driven past I'd realised that she was crying. No, crying is far too small for what she was experiencing. That girl had been pouring her heart out all over the concrete and no one had noticed. Not that there was anyone to notice at two in the morning. But I'd seen. I'd parked the car and gone after her on foot.

"Miss?" I'd cried out.

She'd turned and stopped. I don't look threatening. Never have. I used to be picked on in school for my slight size, but now it is an asset. No one sees me as dangerous. This girl, I could see her sizing me up as I ran toward her, and she made the same mistake as any of the others. She saw not a man but a young boy, fresh-faced and young. In reality I am almost thirty. I did mention that the gods were kind to me.

"Miss?" I said breathlessly. "Are you okay?"

"I'm…" She looked behind me. Probably saw the car.

"I saw you were upset and I worried you'd been attacked," I gabbled out as if I was concerned for her.

"No… I… It's silly really."

Probably. "Oh, I'm sure it isn't. Can I help? Have you been attacked? I can ring the police?"

"No! No, that's okay. I'm just walking home." She sniffed and, in the dim light of the streetlamp, I could see the mix of snot and tears sliding down her face. I didn't stare though. I'd got in trouble for that. Studying people as if they were bugs, it is not the done thing. So instead I smiled and looked in her eyes. They were red rimmed and staring, as if she believed by keeping them open wide I wouldn't notice the build-up of moisture at the corners.

"Where are you going?" I asked.

She took a step back and eyed me warily.

I held up my hands, palms out. See! Look! I am harmless. "Sorry, I just meant I would walk with you to stop anyone hurting you."

She still looked at me oddly, but now it was slightly calculated.

She was thinking that I was not a threat. And she was also thinking that it didn't matter if I was, as she could probably take me. I almost smiled at this. Had she never heard of the stoat? A wonderful creature that kills and eats animals almost three times its own size. Not that I ever eat any of my prey, that would be too weird. But the girl had made up her mind. She stepped toward me, almost crowding. This is another thing people do, trying to assert their dominance. I let her. She nodded at me.

"It's quite a way."

"We can take my car," I said, wondering at her. Had she never heard not to talk to strangers, let alone get in their cars?

"Okay."

And that was it. With one word she signed her own fate. It wasn't as if I coerced her into getting into my car, she went willingly. And now as I stand in my safe house I wonder if it was her box they found. Did she lead them to me?

It had been her sadness I wanted to add. It had been like a piece of broken art in its intensity. Even after she got into the car her eyes continued to leak tears, as if she had no control.

"There should be a tissue in the glove box," I'd said.

"Thank you," she'd mumbled.

"So," I said cheerfully, starting the car. "Where to?"

She'd looked at me oddly and I wondered if I'd let the friendly me slip, and she'd seen the reality. But she didn't. After a moment she told me her road. It was about half an hour away.

"You really shouldn't have tried to walk it."

She'd smiled at my worry.

"What about a cab?"

She'd shrugged. "Ran out of money."

I nodded as if I knew what she was saying. I didn't. I don't think I've ever run out of money. But then I don't think I've ever tried to drink myself into a stupor.

I considered using the chloroform in the side pocket of my door, or the injection in my jacket pocket, but in the end I decided on the more subtle approach and reaching forward I turned on the heated seat.

"Oh," she said, startled.

"Good isn't it?"

She smiled and snuggled down into the warmth. She slipped into sleep quite quickly. I was surprised, but she was tired and a little drunk so it was to be expected. Still, I am always surprised that they fall asleep. After about half an hour of driving I pulled over and reached for the chloroform.

She woke sluggishly. "Are we there?"

I paused then. Her tears had dried on her face and she was just beautiful. "Almost."

Her eyes widened briefly as I placed the cloth over her face. Then her eyes closed and her body went completely limp.

Then I got busy. Even in the safe house I have a variety of little boxes, but that day in the car I'd only had one. She had been difficult to fit in. Why some people let themselves go I don't know. I've always dreamt of having a contortionist girl, one who could get out of the box once I put them in. It never happens though. At some point, no matter how gentle I am there is a snap and I have created art. That girl went into her box and I sat next to her, marvelling at her beauty. Then I left her. In a public place of course. So that she could be admired.

Even I have followers.

But somehow they have found me. My sacrifice for my art is the box. Every girl has her box, and one man. He was the perfect imitation female, and his art made me smile. My dark humour. I have always known that the wooden boxes were traceable, and I guess they found me. Really though, there is no reason to dig up my home.

In the safe house I walk to the top storey and look out. There they are, bringing out the empty boxes. How many had I collected in the house? I don't remember. Some were big enough to be used as side tables in the living room. I always got a kick out of serving people tea on them. The smallest were really only specimen boxes. In the beginning I'd been searching for perfection, but because I couldn't find it, I'd started using parts for my art. The best, I think, were two hands with a beautiful French manicure. I had clasped them in the box, as if she was shaking hands with herself. The rest of the body I'd disposed of. It wasn't needed. Soon though I'd been struck by the waste, and had moved on, making art using the whole body. But those hands were still some of my finest work.

They are bringing out the larger boxes now. Briefly I wonder about turning myself in. I mean it is one thing to create art, but to never get any acknowledgement is tough. Still, nor do I want to be held at her majesty's pleasure, so I turn from the window and go to the smallest bedroom. There is a built in wardrobe and in there is my escape kit. I have never been concerned about money and I'm still not. I have many accounts and many personas. I just have to choose the one I want. Perhaps a change in country or perhaps a move across the world? I can't decide, I'll think on it. Taking off my hoodie and jeans I put on a suit. The quick hum of a shaver and I am as bald as a day-old vulture. I've even removed my eyebrows. It's amazing how different you can look without eyebrows.

Then I leave. As I pass through the alley I can hear the murmur of voices. The neighbours are still at it. Straightening I become the confident businessman with leather satchel and a bag of groceries. As I step into the street I see a neighbour.

"You thinking about buying it?" he asks from across the road. We have shared many a beer together in the evening. But now I pretend he is a stranger.

"Perhaps." My neighbour crosses the road.

"Yeah?"

He is standing only a few feet in front of me. I smile blandly but inside I scream with excitement. This chase is something I live for. "It depends what's going on," I say, nodding to the road and its hidden police cars.

My friend's eyes light up, he so likes to gossip. "There was a serial killer living there and I knew him."

I screw up my nose in distaste. "I'm not sure I would want to buy it. Not with that kind of notoriety."

The man shrugs. "You could get it for a song though."

I tilt my head thoughtfully. I could. "I might just make an offer." I glance at my watch. "Anyway I've got to go. See you around."

He holds up a hand and I can see slight confusion in his face. But he just shrugs and turns. I walk away and can't help but smile. I've got away again, but I have a feeling I am going to need some more boxes. Perhaps a Chinese manufacturer this time, out of the UK. They would be harder to trace.

11 ABSENT RAIN

Shit, I think. I really am not sure about this. I'd been invited on the spur of the moment. My friend had turned to me in the crowded office that always smelled of feet and burnt sugar.

"What are you doing for the bank holiday?"

She'd taken me by surprise. I just sat looked at her. "What?" I'd asked. Truthfully, my head was still wondering if the lady I'd just cold called had really wanted double glazing. I hate that I am one of those people. And I am the worst for hanging up on cold callers, as soon as I hear that tone, the kind that suggests someone is reading from the script. The kind I use every day.

"This holiday? What are you doing?"

My heart sank as I looked at my friend. Honestly, she was the opposite of me in every way. She was blonde and petite, and me, well, let's just say that I don't have to worry about being swamped by suitors, they tend to run a mile. I'd once been told that you have the love life you believe you deserve. In which case I don't like myself much, and I'd decided to do something about it. And one of those things was to get out more. I live alone with no family to speak of. Yet I had to stop myself from shaking my head. Instead I felt compelled to smile and say, "yes."

Rachel had looked surprised and I'd smiled sheepishly. "If that's okay," I added.

She beamed. I mean it wasn't just a smile; it looked as though her face had come alive. "Yes," she'd said, "that would be great."

She'd then drawn a map that had left my head spinning. Which is why I now find myself driving in ever decreasing circles trying to locate what she had assured me was a huge lake.

"So," I say to the empty car, trying to squint through heavy rain, "where is the damn lake?"

The car is obstinately silent. I think I hurt it's feelings about ten miles back when I almost ran off the road trying to read a map and steer at the same time. I wish I'd invested in a sat nav. Invested! That would mean I'd have some cash that was just lying around begging to be spent. Mostly I barely make enough for the bills. This trip has used all my extra cash just on fuel. I am hoping that for the next three days I won't have to go anywhere. I hope to just sit in the sun, turning a bright shade of cherry, but looking at the weather I should have bought my waterproofs.

"I'm sure I've been down this road," I tell the car conversationally. It's still upset. Through the growing dark and driving rain I see a layby. Stopping the car I reach for the nightmare that is the map and try to decipher the scrawl that is Rachel's handwriting.

I shouldn't be in this mess, after all I have a smart phone and it is, well, supposed to be smart. I ought to be flying down the right roads, but as with all smart phones it only keeps its charge for about twenty four hours and it needed recharging about two hours ago. Just to check I pull out the piece of fancy equipment and look at the blank screen, randomly pushing a couple of buttons, about as much help as a brick. Although it probably wouldn't have had signal here anyway. I squint out of the window but all I can see are the shadows of impossibly tall pine trees.

This map has got to be easier to work out. I turn it this way and that. "Any ideas?" Up to this point all I can hear is the constant thud of the rain hitting the roof. My radio has a short in it and a couple of potholes back the little wire had come unstuck, quietening Johnny Cash and leaving me with just the white noise of the road, the rattle of an ill-maintained car and the rain. Now all I can hear is the rain. Turning the map upside down I try to make sense of it. The light has dimmed so much that I turn on the small reading light. My heart is sinking. If I can't find this place in the rain, I don't know how to find it in the dark. Outside I swear I hear a crunch of gravel.

"Come on, Karen, get a grip," I tell myself, feeling a slight shiver of fear. Not apprehension but true fear. My mouth is dry.

The window is dark and steamed up and I use my hand to wipe at the moisture, shivering at the clammy coldness. I peer beyond the gloom, cupping my hands to see. There is something moving out there. Suddenly something smashes into the glass. A hand, fingers outstretched and stiff.

Involuntarily I scream and scoot back in my seat, trapped between the door and the handbrake. Fear makes my mouth gape and air rasp in and out of my lungs. The hand is replaced by a face. One blue eye stares.

"Are you lost?" The question trickles though my consciousness, but I am slow to react. I feel like I'm moving through treacle.

The man raps on the glass using his fist. "Miss, are you alright?" His question is punctuated by claws on the car and a white dog looking at me. "No, Sasha, get down." The face disappears. Finally I feel I am starting to move at the same speed as the rest of the world. He bends down again. "Hello?"

I try to speak but my mouth is completely dry and no sound comes out. I swallow and try again. "Hello?" My voice is weak and a little too high.

He smiles and waves. He has a hood up and rain is tracking down his face. He is soaked. "Are you lost?"

"Yes," I say. "Sorry, you scared me." In my head I wonder at my sudden calming. I understand that it is the dog. I am not scared because he has a huge sloppy Dalmatian. Somewhere in the back of my mind a small voice argues that Cruella had one too, but I ignore it. "Do you know where Still Lake is?"

The man nods. "Which house are you looking for?"

I look down at the map. "Ashdowne House?"

The man's face splits into a grin and I notice that he is missing the left front tooth. "Keep following the road and you will find it." He steps back and, before I can say thanks, he has melted into the shadows. His dog is the last to disappear, its coat glowing in the dark. They don't follow the road but appear to move into the trees.

"Can't be that bad," I inform the car, "he has a dog." I turn the key and she coughs her disapproval before starting, with what I'd like to think was a purr but is more like a persistent cold, phlegmy. The road is hard to see and I crawl along. The rain has stopped to a drizzle but I still feel as if my nose is pressed to the windscreen. In the distance there is a light. At first it just flickers through the trees but soon it is a solid yellow glow and I head toward it, relief relaxing my shoulders and easing the band of pain around my head.

I pull up outside a large house. It is easily the size of a mansion. I'd asked Rachel if I needed a sleeping bag and she'd looked at me blankly. "What for?" she'd asked.

"To sleep."

"Well, you can, but there are plenty of rooms."

"Oh, okay." I'd been shocked, but looking at the house all I can think is, why is Rachel working in the same shit-hole I am? This place has to have at least ten rooms.

I sit and stare. The front of the house is well-lit, as is one window on the second floor. There appear to be four storeys, the last in the roof. The house is made of rough-hewn logs and has a large sweeping porch. Basically it's a dream home. I can see the light and it looks wonderfully inviting, but there is no one opening the door. Surely Rachel would come out to say hi? Maybe she doesn't want me here, but still, she can't just leave me sitting in the drive.

I'm starting to feel a little anxious. As if feeling my worry the car coughs once and then dies. "Shit," I say, jumping in my seat. Reflexively I turn the key and the engine whines but doesn't even cough. I thump the steering wheel. I'll have to go in and at least use the phone, even if I don't stay.

Still, there is no reason someone hasn't come out. I try the key again. Nothing. It's got to be the starter motor. Last time the heap was in the garage the guy in overalls had suggested that I change it, but then I hadn't got the extra £100, so I'd said no. Now it looked like I had no choice. So, it's the house. The warm glow of the windows beckons me. "Maybe they are all around the back." Maybe they have a hot tub. I always wanted to try one. Forcing a smile I get out and reach for my bag and then stop. I'll come back for it once I know everything is alright.

Closing the door I slosh my way to the porch. Luckily it has stopped raining but the drive is one big puddle. I don't see any cars, which is odd, but then there is a garage off to one side, just under the trees, and it looks like it could hold a number of cars. I knock on the door, but after the first touch it swings slightly inwards. The warm light spills out, but I can't help taking a step back. It isn't the light that I try to avoid but the silence. There is no sound, only the occasional drip of the water from the roof of the porch hitting the gravel outside. There isn't even the soft buzz of an abandoned radio. There is just nothing. The door swings wide and I see that it opens onto a large open plan living room. There is a brick built fireplace running through the middle with a large staircase wrapping around the back. The fire isn't out, but it isn't throwing up flames. I can feel the warmth on my face and the smell of cooked chocolate assails me. The smell has just a little bitterness, making me think that the oven may have caught the baking, possibly cookies. I can't see a phone.

The scene reminds me of the pictures I've seen of abandoned houses and colonies, like the cholera island just off the Bronx. The total absence makes me fearful, or perhaps it is fear of what I'll find. I have to go in. I owe Rachel that much at least, after all she has invited me and I owe her just for that. As I stand just outside the reach of the light, only getting an echo of heat, I wonder what is it that I will find.

A small voice reminds me that this family were willing to get to know me better. A slightly stronger voice asks what I think my options are. The truth is I have none. I am too far from anywhere to walk. Where would I go anyway? Find the man with the dog? He just walked into the forest and anyway, now that I look at the situation, why should I trust him? Because he has a dog? I shake my head at the absurdity. The only thing I can do is find out what has gone wrong.

"Rachel?" I call into the still house. There is no answer, but the voice emerging from my throat is small, it will barely carry beyond the front door. Louder, "Rachel?" Nothing. "Anyone?" Still nothing.

I'm going to have to go in. I feel as if my body is being held together with tension. Every muscle is taut and I walk forward stiff-legged as if someone is forcing me. No one is, no one except me. The light engulfs me, first making me squint as my eyes become accustomed to it, then the heat. I hadn't realised how cold I am, but the warmth that wraps itself around me stops the shivering I was hardly aware of. The lack of movement seems to make the silence more absolute. I can't even hear myself.

I'm going to have to do this fast. I don't think my nerves will hold otherwise. I don't know what I'll find and somehow that is more frightening than knowing I may get hurt.

The bitter smell of burning chocolate is worse here. Following it I walk quickly, head swivelling, trying to see some sign of life. I push through. The kitchen is filled with grey smoke. The smell is bitter and acrid. I put a hand over my mouth but it doesn't do much. The smoke is coming from the oven. I open it, expecting flames, but all I see is a shrivelled burnt cake. There is a slight smell of chocolate and I realise that it would have once been perfect. Using an oven mitten that I find on the floor I pull the pan out of the oven and dump it into the sink. I then go to the back door and open it. The smoke immediately begins to leave the room, although the cloying smell remains. The kitchen is white and on the island are two glasses. One sits upright and is filled with a red liquid, the other is on its side and, looking at the spill of red, it must have been at least half full. No one appears to have tried to clean it up. It is as if they just disappeared. The glass standing upright has a red lipstick smear like some lost lover's mark.

Briefly I look out of the door. Although I can hear the trees creak I can't see anything but night. I close the door and reach for the lock. There is no key and a quick look around doesn't reveal one, so I just leave the door. I suppose that I could rummage in drawers but it seems somehow rude. Still, as I turn my back I feel vulnerable.

I move back to the living room. It really is lovely. There are three huge cream sofas, one of which turns a corner. It's the kind of sofa that I want to own, one day. In the middle is a fake bear rug, at least I hope it's fake. I step around it just in case. There are a pile of blocks near the head of the rug. Four are piled on top of one another and it looks like they could fall at any point. I carefully step around them. There is a closed door off the room and a quick peep in shows a coat room. I recognise the pink fluffy abomination that Rachel loves, even though it always smells of wet dog. The hooks are full. They left without their coats? Perhaps they were taken?

The stairs are wide and I walk cautiously up them, trying to be silent. I know I ought to cry out or make a noise but it is my instinct to hide, not to draw attention to myself. What if the person who took them is still here? I know that it's a silly idea. Perhaps a man could snatch one or two, but Rachel had said that there would be at least six adults and two children. They have to be hiding or they must have left for some reason. The first floor is a series of rooms and most of the doors are open; all are bedrooms and all empty. Each room has a selection of bags and suitcases, some open and some closed, but abandoned awaiting their people. The last door is closed and I can hear water. I push on the door and it resists a little and then eases open. I squeeze in as soon as there is room.

Like the kitchen, the bathroom is white, glaringly so. I wince at the light. The floor is soaking wet with about an inch of water. The only reason it hasn't escaped is that the room is a little sunken. It's a wet room. But the drain is blocked and the bath taps are turned on. I've never seen a wet room so I'm not sure if there ought to be a bath, but there is one. I reach down to turn off the taps and see a face in the water. Stumbling back I scream. The scream becomes a gasp as I sit in the puddle that is the floor. Apart from the drip of the excess water escaping from the bath there is no sound. I whimper, the sound escaping despite my intention to remain silent. Quickly I scramble to my feet reaching for the door. But the face... I have to look. I have to see who it is. Going over I stare down and see blond hair flowing in the water, blue eyes staring up at me. Except it is wrong. There is no body and no blood. It is just a head in the bottom of the bath. Rolling up a sleeve I reach in and, grasping the wiry strands, I pull. In my hand is a head, but not of a person, of a doll. Berating myself for being so silly I pull the plug and watch the water start to slip away. The doll's head in my hand is creeping me out so I place it on the floor. The plug in the floor of the room appears to be blocked by a flannel. I remove it and the drain gives a gurgling discharge as if defiant against the water that rushes down its throat. Turning back I notice that a wet towel was the reason the door had been so hard to move. I pick it up thinking of hanging it on the hook. Except there is no hook. My brow ruffles. How had it got there? I would understand if it had fallen but there is nowhere for it to fall. I turn a slow circle. I'm alone. I look up. The light is so very bright. There, next to the light, is a hand print. How? I turn off the light and give a panicked yelp as the room is plunged into darkness.

I flick the switch. Nothing. I could have sworn I saw a handprint. It had been hard to see but it had been there and it had been brown. Blood dries brown. It had been on the ceiling. My brain stalls as I try to ask how. My breath is wheezing in and out of my throat, the air hurts. The darkness is absolute. I should be able to see from the light in the hall and living room. Reaching behind me I grasp the door and slip back out into the hall. I have no idea where the light switch is. I can't even remember how many rooms there are. I shuffle forward, whimpering and gasping. I've got to stop otherwise I won't hear. What if someone is behind me?

I whip round with my arms thrown wide and a scream tearing out of me. As I do the hall is flooded with light. All the lights are on, even in the rooms that had no light earlier. Turning, I fly down the stairs and toward the front door. In my peripheral vision I notice that the four blocks are no longer piled on top of each other but scattered as if something has pushed them over. I run; the door is open and I plough through. Getting in my car I reach for the key. It's still there. I turn it saying a prayer. Nothing. Oh god, please.

I turn it and the engine catches. It growls and then holds. I put the car into first and ease up on the clutch. The engine whines, but I am not moving. "Please car," I whisper. She seems to hear and chugs forward a couple of feet and then dies.

I scream and turn the key. Nothing. "Please God, start," I pray. A hand slams into the side of the car making the window spider web. I yell and move away from it. Through the fuzzy glass I see someone and I hear a low laugh.

"It's no good praying, he can't help you now," and he smiles. His tooth is missing. I don't see his dog. Curling in on myself I whimper. I go where I will be safe. To that place everyone has but few venture. From this green field I hear glass breaking and I feel myself floating. Abstractedly I realise my face becomes wet. I think it's raining.

12 FEAR

To begin with no one was afraid of him. I know I wasn't. He was odd but he'd talk to everyone in the street. Dad knew him well and sometimes I'd wander over and have a chat with them.

"You're a good girl, aren't you," he'd say, his voice high. I'd just nod and hide behind my father. They'd then go back to talking about cars or how Paul across the road was always cleaning his.

"He's very odd," Martin would say and Dad would nod his agreement, as they watched Paul give the car another wash, the soap suds removing the last speck of dust from the metallic silver paint. It was when he started hoovering the engine that Dad would roll his eyes and Martin would say in that funny high voice, "Very odd." I laugh now, for Martin to think Paul odd. I even smiled back then, but only to be polite.

No one had a problem with Martin, but I found him strange. His voice was too high and he would swing his shoulders as he walked but keep the rest of his body completely rigid. The kids would follow him as he made his way up and down the street, my sister one of them, her arms held out at her sides and her hands limp, moving her shoulders exaggeratedly from one side and then the other. They would mince behind him and he would laugh and make his own steps even more strident, leaving the kids giggling and falling about in his wake. But that laugh never reached his eyes. To me he always seemed to be holding a secret, one he had no intention of telling. Except every now and then he would look at me and it was as if he wanted to tell me his secret. Then he would sidle up and whisper, "Are you still a good girl, Joanne?" I'd nod and run off home. It got to the stage that I would just disappear if I saw him.

It was his eyes. They would stare at you like those of a shark;

dead, but at the same time calculating. As if he was trying to see if I was a truly good on the inside, or if I was stained. To begin with I found him unsettling and then annoying, but eventually this man induced fear.

He was always clean shaven with freshly pressed clothes and his hair was neatly combed and parted down the middle. It caught the light as if it were patent leather and I remember asking Dad about it one day after Martin had just left. He had shrugged and said it was probably some sort of cream or oil.

Martin only touched me a couple of times; once to shake hands and the other to pat my arm. Both I remember distinctly. The handshake had been limp and his hand cold, but at the same time clammy, so that by the end I felt I needed to wipe my hand on my jeans to get him off. I didn't. I'm too polite. The second time I'd been upset and not looking where I was going. It was some sort of fight between friends and I was just storming up the road to my house. I wasn't paying attention. If I had been then perhaps I would have stopped and taken another, longer route. I would have missed Martin, but with my eyes to the ground I didn't see him until it was too late.

"Joanne, are you alright?" he'd asked, standing in front of me and blocking my way. I just nodded. He put out a hand and patted my arm. Actually, it was more like a stroke. Inside I shuddered but on the outside I refused to show him any reaction. Instead I looked at the ground and allowed the tears to fall. "You on your way home?" I nodded, staying quiet. "Do you want me to walk you?" I shook my head, thinking, please, no. One more cold clammy stroke and he moved out of the way. I didn't wait but strode off as fast as I could. After a moment I heard his steps retreating and I relaxed a little, only then realising how tense I'd been.

That was the last time I saw Martin before the police pulled into the road. I suppose he was on the news, but I didn't watch it. So it came as a surprise when a line of cop cars and a van pulled up outside his house. I hadn't seen him in a while, but really that had been a blessing. The police pulled up and broke into his house. The door was one of those panelled ones and as the metal battering ram connected, it just folded in. All of us kids just stood with our mouths open until the parents cottoned onto what was happening and then they came and got us.

I then had to rely on a gift I have. In olden days children were seen and not heard, and I had worked out that if you sit quietly and pretend to read, adults forget you are there. That is what I did to find out about Martin.

Mum was in the living room with her friend Miriam, so I just sat really quietly with a book. Neither of them even looked at me.

"I can't believe it," Miriam started.

"He seemed so nice," Mum finished, and I was intrigued, not that I'd ever thought Martin nice.

"I know his mother. They've pulled down her new conservatory and dug up the foundations." Miriam's voice rose. "All because he helped put it up."

"But do you think he did it?" Mum asked.

"Killed all those women?"

"And cut them up," Mum added.

Miriam shrugged. "I don't know. If you'd asked me before all this I would have said no, but now..." she tailed off.

I sat there for the rest of Miriam's visit, unseen, but all they talked about was the kids and the weather. Once Miriam had left Mum stopped inside the living room and looked at me. "Don't tell the younger kids."

I turned innocent eyes to her and she just smiled and shook her head. I didn't tell anyone, but I think I must have been the only person in the street who wasn't surprised at Martin's gruesome dealings. He had killed prostitutes and sometimes I still hear his question, "are you a good girl?"

PRAGMA

to shop for a knight

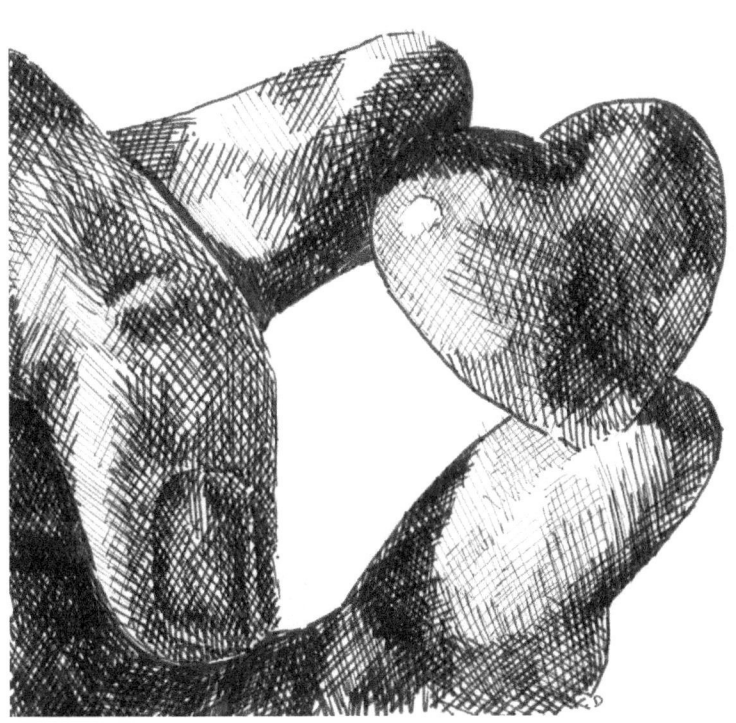

13 BE CAREFUL WHAT YOU WISH FOR

"Get it straight!" May told Lucy.

"I am!" She argued back.

"You didn't last week and Chuck noticed, said my legs looked bandy."

"Shit, he never did?"

"Yeah," May said with a sigh, "but," her face lightened with a grin, "he might bring some stockings."

"Really?" Lucy said hopefully.

"My stockings," May said, trying to give Lucy a stern look and keep totally still.

Lucy just sighed and grimaced at the slight wobble near May's ankle. Still, if she got some stockings she wouldn't need to have the seam line drawn into the back of her leg. Lucy sat back and looked up. "Done."

"Let me see." But no sooner had she spoken then the doorbell rang. Jumping May got off the low coffee table, straightened her pencil skirt and grabbed the jacket off the back of the chair. "Night," she threw back as she slipped on her shoes and left.

Lucy sat for a moment and sighed. Being the sister of such a dynamic character was interesting but trying at the same time. She got to her feet and walked to the little kitchen. Moving out of their parents' home had been an adventure but now she was tired of being alone and not for the first time she wished she was a little more outgoing. Still, she liked her life; they both worked in the munitions factory and she found it exciting and dangerous, even though she was doing the same thing every day. But May seemed to be more interested in men, like Chuck; he was handsome enough, actually Lucy thought him beautiful. He was American, he had to be with a name like Chuck, so he had access to chocolate and such, but Lucy couldn't see where it would go. May loved him. If fact she loved him more than anything and Lucy knew it was likely Chuck would pop the question soon. Would that mean that she would move out to America? Lucy couldn't see Chuck settling down here, all he did was complain about the weather and the fact that *everything was grey*. What did he expect? They were at war.

Putting the kettle on the hob Lucy was surprised to hear the front door open. Through the closed door of the kitchen she could hear voices. May and some guy, definitely not Chuck. This guy was London through and through.

"Let's sit you down," a gruff voice said.

May was definitely crying. Leaving the kettle Lucy walked into the living room. "May?"

"He… He…" May's sobs made understanding her impossible.

Lucy turned to the young man, noting his scruffy appearance and flat cap. This guy wasn't in the army or navy, had he not been called up? He was familiar as well. Lucy thought she'd seen him talking to May a couple of times in the factory. Still it was odd that he was here. "Where's Chuck?" she asked May, but didn't take her eyes off the man in front of her.

May's sobs got louder and she curled into a foetal position on the chair. The guy put a hand on her head in comfort. "I was at the bar," he said. "She was with an American."

"Chuck," Lucy interrupted.

The man nodded. "He gave her a ring."

"Oh, May!" Lucy said eyes alight with laughter. Then she looked at her sister and the happiness faded. "What happened?"

"There was a condition."

"To move to America?"

"Yes, that, and no children."

"What?" Lucy said, shocked. "No children? But May..."

She stopped suddenly, aware that she was talking to a stranger. He seemed to realise as well.

"I'll go," he said. "Can I call tomorrow and make sure she's all right?"

Lucy shrugged, kneeling next to May. "If you want."

"Thank you," he said quietly and left. Neither heard the door click closed.

Lucy held May until she had stopped sobbing uncontrollably. Later that night sitting in their nighties with a hot chocolate each, Lucy turned to May. "Who is he?"

"Who?" May asked, gazing into her hot chocolate as if looking for a meaning to everything.

"The other guy who helped you home."

May gave a wan and wistful smile. "George".

"And George is?"

"He works at the factory."

"I thought I recognised him," Lucy said. "He hasn't been called up?"

May shook her head. "He has asthma."

Lucy nodded. "He knows you well?"

"Just as friends."

Sighing, Lucy decided to ask about Chuck, risking sending May into another downward spiral. "What happened?"

"He walked me home. I was upset."

"No, what happened with Chuck?"

"It was like George said. Chuck doesn't want children. Or rather he can't."

"Can't?"

"He had himself fixed so he couldn't. Turns out there is some sort of illness runs in the family."

"Why d'you say no?"

May sipped her drink before answering. "I want children."

"But you love him so much," Lucy said, frowning.

May smiled at her. "I do, but I want a family, a proper family, with children." May leaned forward. "Do you understand?"

"I suppose. But Chuck loves you as much."

May leaned back. "So does George."

Lucy blinked. "So? You love Chuck."

"But George wants kids too."

Lucy closed her eyes and said nothing. After a moment May got up. "I'm off to bed." She paused in the doorway. "What do you want?"

Lucy didn't look at her but at her now empty cup. "To be loved."

"Children?"

"If it's in my future then yes, if not then so be it."

May shook her head. "You don't understand."

Lucy looked at the confusion etched on her face. "No, I don't."

14 THE COUNT

I was bullied in school. Not just the pushing and slapping kind of bullying but the all-out outcast bullying. I was the kid standing in the corner. I was the kid to be picked last and I was the child who if others touched, they would wipe their hands on their clothes to get rid of the 'lurgy'. Every school playground has one and I was it. Now of course I would be remiss to say that I don't hold them any malice. I mean it would be pointless now, what with me pushing up daisies and all.

Pushing up daisies, that is an odd phrase. Actually I am sitting in a resin urn on my mother's bottom shelf in her cupboard, just below her favourite jumper and next to her best knickers. I have no idea why she has popped me in here, but it is deserved I suppose as I barely knew her once she was in this delightful apartment. I'm hoping that it's because of the urn. I am fairly fastidious and the plastic finish looks nothing like the wood it is trying to emulate. I was hoping it would be a brass urn. In fact I'd even put it in the will, but when she went to the undertaker he had looked down his rather long nose at her.

"Brass will tarnish," he had said in a disagreeable nasal voice.

"That is what he wanted," my mother said, wringing her hands together and not meeting his eyes.

"It will tarnish." Now the undertaker used that 't' like a shot from a gun and my mother actually flinched. Right there I wished I could help her, but the truth is that in life I was no better than her; a drip of a man in lank suits with thinning hair. So I wasn't surprised when she went for the over-priced wood-effect urn. Nor was I surprised at the smug smile that crossed his face as my mother walked away, her red hands pushed into her coat pockets. What I was surprised at was the anger directed toward her and not him.

I was an only child. Mother had to raise me alone after my father fell from a building during its construction. I understand that health and safety were non-existent then but really, how do you fall from a ten storey building when you ought to be tied in? I sometimes wonder if she drove him to it. It isn't that my mother is a bad woman, if anything she is too nice. I saw a neighbour catch her outside once and ask if she wouldn't mind shining his shoes because he was out of polish. Most people would have thrown him the polish and told him to do it himself. Not my mum. She walked into the house with the shoes and set out the kit in front of her. I watched her meticulously line up the polish and brushes.

"Mum, you could have given him the polish."

She just shook her head and started to spread the thick black cream over the surface. "He would have done it wrong."

"He would have done it his way."

She just shook her head and took another clockwise swipe of the cloth in to the tin to coat it with polish and then rub it in quick clockwise circles onto the shoe. She was doing this with familiarity.

"Mum, you done this often?"

"Sometimes."

It was then that I realised that my mother was vulnerable and that she seemed happy in her misery. Maybe that is a little harsh but really she would never stick up for herself, not over shoes or my urn. And then of course there were the hands. I used to look at my friends' mother's hands and see they were beautifully soft and elegant. Then my mother's; all red and chapped, cracking around the knuckles. I once counted how many times she washed her hands whilst making a sandwich; twenty. I think that's what made my dad walk off the scaffolding. My mother would clean up before the dirt appeared. He used to sit on the sofa and watch her polish or scrub the floor on her hands and knees, just like her mother had taught her.

"You don't have to," he would say. And she would pause before going back to her task.

"But I must."

Father would then get up and leave the room. Of course I was only five at the time, but I remember him leaving. That was the main thing I remember about him, his leaving. I can still see his broad back and smell his aftershave; a strange mix of sharp lemon and musk. As I grew I had a feeling that the sharp lemon had rubbed off from mother; she loved the smell of lemons. Even to the end I would hear the heavy foot of a man, a four beat and then a slight hitch and I would look up expecting to see a checked shirt and smell that odd scent. But he had left us by the time I was six, leaving me to my mother's mercies.

That makes it sound as if I was abused, and I wasn't. If anything Mother kept too close a watch on me. She would want to know where I was at all times.

"Joseph, where are you going?" she would call.

"Out," would be my answer, although I was normally going to the cinema, alone. But the pictures were on Mother's 'not-to-go-ever' list. I think it was the sticky floor; that comforting carpet that would tug at your shoes as if trying to stop you leaving. But it could also have been overflowing bins or the smell of burnt popcorn. All of which I relished. It was on one of my jaunts that I saw the woman I was destined to marry.

I would love to say that our eyes met and it was love at first sight, a real movie moment. But the reality is that she saw me in my ironed shirt and trousers with creases just so and turned to her friends, her hand covering her mouth. Their quick, you-can't-see-me glances and guffaws of laughter made my shoulders slump and my eyes turn to the red carpet, hoping that it would turn to quicksand. It didn't, but as the years turned I noticed that her group got smaller and smaller. My weekly routine never varied and one day whilst buying the too-sweet popcorn she came over.

"Do you mind if I sit with you?"

"Of course not," I said, but what I really meant was – will you marry me? Although I didn't ask that question until five years passed; until mother went into a home. I was not taking my Josie to see her, not after the last time.

I had been eleven and I'd triumphantly taken a girl home, a little thing lower on the school social scale than me.

"Mother, I brought a friend home," I said.

"A friend?" She had sounded so surprised that Miriam had looked at me, as if something was wrong with me. I smiled.

"Of course," I said, taking Miriam's hand and trying to ignore the clammy wetness of it.

Mother had walked in then and screamed. Not a half-hearted scream but a full blown cry of fear and hurt. "Don't!" she yelled and pointed at our entwined hands.

Miriam immediately let go and slipped from my grasp. In fact she didn't stop, but turned and was out of our immaculate white door in minutes.

I had turned hurt eyes to my mother as I followed Miriam out.

"Wait..."

But she was running. Across the road my peers laughed and pointed. "What's wrong, gross boy?" they called. I slunk back inside to find my mother on her hands and knees scrubbing the patch of floor Miriam had been standing on.

"Nasty, dirty bitch," she was mumbling under her breath.

"What?"

She had jumped when she saw me watching. "She was dirty," she said simply, as if that was the only answer I needed.

"No she wasn't."

She had nodded and then her eyes had fallen to my hand, the one that had been holding Miriam's hand. Her face became cold and hard, and for a moment she had seemed unlike my mother. In that moment I had been scared of her. I think I even flinched as she grabbed me, by the wrist and not the hand, and dragged me into the kitchen. There, before I could brace myself, she had plunged my hand into the water. Except as I smelt the ammonia I realised that this wasn't water.

I had fought her and the liquid had done the damage. Two days later I had gone to the doctor with a strange red hand, a chemical burn he had said. No shit! I said. How did I get it? Well, I just shrugged. She was still my mother and she was not right in the head. There, in the doctor's waiting room, I decided not to be like her. I would not be as crazy. But of course by then I was already lost. There were fifteen chairs, twenty four magazines and it had taken me 6 and three-quarter steps to reach the chair I had sat in. I was counting.

I had been counting for as long as I could remember. It must have started as a teaching aid, something my parents did to make sure I had a head start in school.

"Look at the cows in the field. How many are there?"

That sort of thing, but by the time I was ten it was a fixture and the reason behind the bullying, apart from my mother. I would count to school, to the classroom, to my desk, to the blackboard; it was a compulsion. Then I would just count paces. In fact it stayed like that for quite a while. When I met Josie I was still counting, but I would do it silently. Gone were my days of loudly crying out my steps. Now I could hold conversations and follow them whilst still continuing my silent mantra. Josie never realised I was different, that I had a problem, not until it escalated, and by then we had been married for five years.

My wife was the dearest woman I ever knew. She never questioned my waiting for my mother to leave before we married and she never accused me of being distant. Well she did, but not until much later, not until we were taking verbal blows. She accepted me and my minimalistic lifestyle. But the pressures of life were part of me; the mortgage and the constant worry of Josie not having a child. They wore away at my veneer of normalcy until my true crazy shone though, bright blue and easy for all to see.

It started small. One day I straightened all the small crystal animals that were on the mantel in the living room. Josie watched me.

"I'm trying to watch television," she complained, her tiny feet tucked under her, giving her a childish air.

"I'm almost done."

She sighed. "Is this about the child?"

We had never discussed it, apart from me vaguely mentioning that Spring that it would be nice to have a child. My hand froze on a small crystal bear sitting up with a tiny crystal pink bow.

"Because I have decided not to have any."

And there it was, the decision that I was hoping she would never make.

"Why?"

"Does there have to be a reason?"

"Yes."

"I want to keep my figure, and anyway I like our life too much. I don't want to ruin it."

I had closed my hand around that small animal, all cold and sharp, and turned to her. "But…"

"No."

There was no sense in arguing. It was at this point that I showed an aggression that I felt bad about afterwards. I opened my hand and the bear fell in a slow deadly path to our inset marble fire surround. She watched it and her mouth had grown wide and circular, like a cartoon character. I watched and felt nothing. I had created this normal veneer to give my wife everything and all I asked for in return was a child. She was denying me that. So why not show her what she had married?

The bear hit the surface of the marble and shattered. The noise was like a gunshot and I remember her echoing scream. Then I was on my knees picking up the shards. Thirty pieces; it seemed appropriate. I went over and handed them to her. She took them and I clasped my hands around hers. I squeezed and relished her sound of pain.

"Whatever your decision is."

I then sat in my seat ignoring her sobs and her leaving. It is the only time I ever asserted myself.

The next time I ever had any relationship with her was when a lawyer was present. That was when I found out that she thought me distant and odd. That she wouldn't have ever had a child with me, not for all my money. Then of course she had held out her hand and demanded half. I'd given it to her, no questions as long as she signed an affidavit to never mention the bear. She had. Money was no problem, I was a banker and my untimely death occurred before the crash, so there was never an issue.

The first time I walked back into the house and it was all mine, I got out the cleaning products. I had to get rid of any sign of her. So I washed away my Josie and at some point it became as important as the counting. But that had changed as well. I had become obsessed with odd numbers. So much so that I would walk an extra step to land on that holy grail of an odd number. It made me feel better. I didn't realise but right then I signed my own death warrant. The number twenty nine started to appear. I loved to count to twenty nine. My work suffered. And one year to the day after Josie's settlement payment I was asked by my empolyer to take a leave of absence.

"For how long?" I asked.

My boss, a wiry man of greys, had laced his long fingers together. "Indefinitely."

And that was that. I didn't need the job. I had enough money to live two lifetimes, but the human contact was something I couldn't do without. Except I had to.

I suppose it was around this time that my killer was also coming into his own. He had chosen his profession well. My small act of violence was nothing compared to his. By the age of ten he had already killed a man. You have to realise that on the streets of the city, there are other rules, harsher rules. I was a suburb inhabitant and even I knew that the city was more savage. The homeless would just disappear, and it was on these that Dean honed his craft. He was quick and effective. By the age of sixteen his life path was set, as was mine.

My life had become a world of counting and lemon freshness. I was my mother and so much more. I had my own insecurities which I piled onto hers. I relished my difference. If I had told Josie the truth I believed we would have had a child. The fact that she would never have dated me in the first place was lost on me. Instead I saw only what I wanted to see and I jumped to my own conclusions. By giving in to my desires I was showing the world who I was. Except I never saw the wrongness; instead I got worse.

Six years later and the day of my death I woke to a pitch black room. I had found that even a chink of light could keep me awake. Moonlight was my enemy. Josie used to dance in it and stare in wonder at the pale blue-white globe, so I shunned it. My curtains were blackout and velcroed to the wall. A wonderful invention that allowed them to be pulled and used normally, but at night they became my barrier. In my pitch black room all I could hear was the soft ticking of my clock and the soft hum of the immersion heater. I emerged from my sanctuary to the ensuite, turning on the dim light, which seemed so bright every morning. It was four o'clock and I knew that I needed to rush to get out to the centre for nine.

You see, by now I was counting about everything. How many steps to the door? Then down the stairs to the kitchen, which would need a clean before I used it. You can't be too careful of germs. Then wash my already red and stinging hands. I had chemical burns on both hands now, but I would nurture this pain and even add to it with every brush of an alkaline cleaning product, scented with lemon freshness. I was even doing the dishes in a little bleach, diluted of course, but you can't be too careful.

At the same time Dean was up and around, getting his latest hit list from the local tyrant. Mostly it was bums and the homeless, but that day I was on the list. You see, said local tyrant had been at school with me, and was now my Josie's new husband. One day he had taken her hand in his, her scarred palm turned up. Until that moment she had said nothing about me and he had been willing to let it slide. I mean, his past was not something he wanted to discuss with her so why should he insist she discuss hers?

That day though she had been suffering from arthritis caused from the scars in her palm. She once held her hand up to me in the court and I had seen the extent of the damage. I don't remember the blood or the screams, just a feeling of empowerment. It turns out though that she had some nerve damage and one tiny piece of crystal had become lodged behind a delicate part, too hard to remove. She had accused and right there in the court I had smiled.

"There you are, Sweetie, you can take me wherever you go."

She had screamed and lunged for me. If they hadn't held her back I think she might have actually tried to hurt me. But that sentence had played on her mind and that morning she had been unable to sleep, just rock and hold her hand away from her body. Her gentle giant of a husband had held her and insisted on the story. He had said he would take care of it and put my name on the list, the list that Dean carefully folded and placed in his pocket.

"You want me to stake out the banker before I take care of him?"

"No, and make it ugly."

My fate was sealed. As I closed the front door for the twenty ninth time, I gave Dean just enough time to park the car and get out. He straightened his suit and started to walk towards my block. We were separated by a hundred yards and a corner. I walked with head down, counting. He walked with head up, as alert as a lion on the savannah. He saw me and knew my face; the wonders of the web. He got out the knife and stopped maybe five feet away.

I didn't notice him until I saw his feet in my limited field of vision. I actually thought, nice shoes, and then I looked up. He smiled, stepped forward and plunged the knife into my stomach, cutting through the large bowel and the small intestine. Pulling out the knife he turned and walked away. Before he left though he gave me a small crystal bear, with a perfect pink bow.

15 THE RESCUE

And so they came to Ballybunion, Gerry and Julie, with the brackish wind rushing and, in the street, crowds of brutish men were gathering.

"Are you sure, Gerry?"

"Yes," he said tensely. He didn't turn to look at Julie, but she turned to him, noting his slumped stance and pale complexion. For just a moment she felt sorry for him and then an ice blast of rain hit her face and the whole day came crashing down on her. She stifled a cry and turned from her husband of five years to gaze with a blank expression at the men gathering. She couldn't believe that they were going to place their trust and hope in the hands of a group that looked as if they were better suited to pouring out of a pub on a Saturday night. One of the men caught her glance and whatever he saw made him begin to amble over, his gait slow and rolling, like a man who had spent too much time on the sea.

"Missus, you okay?" he asked and glanced briefly at the man next to her. They both needed somewhere warm and dry to sit down. He was fairly certain that they were in shock, but then he wasn't surprised. If his children had gone missing with a storm this big about to break on the east coast he would be worried. Hell, he'd be tearing his hair out. That was what got him concerned. They should be worried or pacing or something, but they stood in the weather still and quiet, as if they already thought the children long gone. Unless they knew something he didn't. The children were lost and they were within the golden hour for finding them. Weren't they?

"I'll be back in a minute," Cal said and then turned back to the group. Jogging over he caught the captain's attention. "Sir, I don't like it. They," he indicated behind him, "aren't acting right."

The larger man looked over Cal's shoulder and nodded. "I see it."

"I'm gonna take them to McMunn's, get them warm and then see if I can get their story." Both men now glanced at the distraught couple. They were turned away from each other as if they were strangers and not married at all. Perhaps they didn't get on, but he was surprised at the extreme posture. Normally these situations brought people together. Normally they supported each other, but these people didn't. Just what was going on?

The captain remained silent for a moment and then nodded. "Okay, Cal. But take a radio. We're going to start out as soon as the stragglers arrive. We'll take the coastal path as that's where the father said they were going."

Cal looked confused. "Sir, its dark and we're meant to be in the hour of them going missing? Who lets their kids wander around at night?"

The captain looked at Cal and shrugged. "I don't know. Get what you can and let me know."

Cal nodded and returned to the couple. "I've got us somewhere warm to sit and wait." Both adults turned and followed Cal's broad figure as he walked them to the pub. Holding the door open he waited while they went inside, still acting as complete strangers. He nodded to the barman as they passed and Cal showed them into a private area. He actually hated this room. It was meant to be for business meetings but he found the red and brown herringbone carpet wearing on the eyes. Luckily though John, the owner, had popped a large over-stuffed sofa along the far wall. It was this that the parents went to and immediately sat on, at opposing ends, neither removing any clothing nor acknowledging the other's presence. Cal grabbed a chair from the many around the boardroom table that graced the middle of the room. Boardroom table indeed. It was actually an old dining room table with multiple chairs picked up from the local auctions. Still, Cal had heard business men actually complimenting John on his 'quaint' room, with its rustic charm. He just saw it as a mismatch of furniture items picked for their low value, but then some called him a cynic. He popped the chair next to the sofa and slung himself across it.

"Do you need anything?" he asked. They both briefly glanced at him and then shook their heads. No, this couple were not acting the same as others he had come across. "So how did Abby and Bea go missing?" Normally he would have asked a lot of leading questions before he got to the 'what happened' stage but somehow he knew that these people were not going to talk. In fact neither showed signs of saying anything. Cal sighed and removed his coat, which, designed for mountain rescue, was stifling in the pub's atmosphere. "Look, you have to tell me something. Those kids need to be found and anything will help." He paused and waited. The woman, Julie, looked at him and she seemed not worried but tired and resigned. The man, on the other hand, would not meet his eye and just sat slouched at the end of the sofa. He appeared to make himself as small as possible. Cal was about to start again when there were raised voices from outside. Cal saw the handle turn and open. The town's one and only full time policeman walked in, shaking the rain off his jacket as he came. Just as the door closed Cal saw the barman appear behind with a mop and morosely begin cleaning up.

"Cal."

"Frank."

Frank took in the couple and Cal allowed his gaze to wander back to them. Why hadn't they asked about the kids? Surely the presence of the policeman suggested that there might be news but although the woman watched him, the man showed no reaction. Julie even appeared tense and ill-at-ease. What was going on?

"Would this be Mr and Mrs Lander?" Frank asked, looking into his notebook.

Neither responded so Cal answered for them. "No, this is Julie Smith and Gerry Jones."

"Really," Frank said and rolled his eyes, "Smith and Jones? I don't think so. Have you any ID on you?"

The man stirred slightly and said, "It wasn't our fault."

"Gerry, no!" Julie said, turning to her partner fully and shaking her head. "Just stay quiet!"

The man looked at her with contempt. "No, I won't stay quiet. What about Abby and Bea?"

"So the children exist?" Frank asked.

Gerry nodded and wrung his hands together, keeping his eyes on the floor. "We aren't supposed to have them, but they arrived early."

Julie sighed loudly and turned her attention to the two confused men in front of her. "We had no choice. I was against the idea from the start."

Cal's eyes darted to Gerry as he barked a laugh. "Yeah right. Little Miss White as Snow."

"I didn't say that," the woman shouted. "It's just that I didn't think it was a good idea."

"It was your idea to come here!" Gerry cried.

She suddenly fell silent and just shrugged.

"Okay," Cal said. "Firstly, what do you mean 'they arrived' and why was there no choice?"

"Cal," Frank said, placing a hand on his shoulder, "let me ask the questions. You can stay in case there is anything for the rescue team but please stay quiet."

Cal blinked in confusion but nodded his agreement.

"Who are you?" Frank asked pulling up a chair and sitting near Cal but effectively blocking the exit for the couple.

"Gerry and Julie," the girl said.

"And who are you to Abby and Bea?"

"No one really," Julie said with a shrug.

"You kidnapped them?" Cal asked, his voice higher and strident.

"Cal, please." Frank said with a frown.

Sheepishly Cal settled back in his seat and tried to appear calm although his heart was beating far too fast. Now not only did they have to find the kids but they could be in deep trouble.

"You were saying?" Frank said turning to Julie, but Gerry answered.

"We didn't mean to take them but they'd been left."

"Left?" Frank said, scribbling into his book.

"Yes, we live on a council estate and there's this family. You know the type…" Gerry stopped and looked around the quaint pub, "or maybe you don't. Anyway they have two kids and they just leave them. We had been watching, so when they went away on holiday and left them…" He fell silent and Julie finished.

"We took them. The damn parents had decided to leave them, like in the sodding movie, Home Alone."

"Jesus," Cal said.

"Exactly."

"Right, this makes things complicated," Frank said. "When did the kids go missing?"

"This morning," Gerry said quietly and shuffled in his seat.

They all jumped as Cal's radio hissed and crackled into the room. "Sorry." He walked out trying to get a better signal.

Finally, *Cal?*

"Yes?"

We've made it down to the nine daughters and there are signs that someone's fallen in.

"Shit."

That's our thought. Better let the parents know it is touch and go.

"They aren't the parents."

What?

"Turns out they snatched two kids because they'd been left. They've given false names…"

Yeah I wondered about Smith and Jones. Okay, well find out anything you can. We're going down but if they fell from here…

"I know there isn't much that can be done."

Hey… We only find them…

Cal sighed, "Okay. Over and out." He didn't know why people came here. They were probably hiding. Trying to give the kids a new start or a taste of family life. Good intentions, the route to bad consequences. Still, he understood their theory. If the family had left them then who would notice if they were at home alone or having a holiday in Ireland. Turning to go back into the pub he just wished they hadn't picked Ballybunion. As he walked in Frank was moving out.

"You leaving them?" Cal asked.

"Yeah," Frank said. "Where are they going to go? They're both wracked with guilt. Any sign of the girls?"

"It doesn't look good. The captain says there are signs they were around the nine daughters."

Frank winced. He lived here and the nine daughter's hole gave him the creeps. Every windy day the whole place would cry. It sounded like a woman trapped. "Do they think they went down?"

"Possibly." Cal shivered. "I'm going to get my coat and then I'll go out and join the others. Missing kids in this weather is not good. At least we've found some sign but I don't know…. What do I tell the couple?"

"By rights nothing. They aren't related."

Cal nodded. "What possessed them?"

"Who knows… Just wish they'd kept an eye on them better."

"How did the kids get away?"

"They woke this morning about ten and thought that the kids were still asleep. It was quiet, but they'd gone. Didn't realise till about an hour later." Frank shrugged. "They'll throw the book at them. Especially if the girls are harmed."

"Jesus." Cal shook his head. "I feel sorry for the kids out there and the folk in the pub. What you up to now?"

"Make a couple of phone calls then I'll be back to arrest them."

"Jesus."

"I know." With that Frank walked away waving a hand in the air.

Cal picked up the radio, "Captain?"

Yeah. What's up, Cal?

"The kids have been missing since before 10 am."

Jesus.

"I'm on my way out. Any sign?"

None. I'll increase the search area and call in more help.

"Okay. See you in about fifteen minutes."

With a sigh Cal pushed open the pub door and felt the warmth of the pub, except it did nothing to warm his chilled body. It was going to be a long night.

AGAPE

to give all and ask for no return

16 DEVOTION

I think I might have done something wrong. Look, there is the milkman, trying to look in again. It was only that I was worried about the milk going off. I know, Alfred. I understand that it might not get any easier but I had to tell him. You know I hate to twist the cap off the bottle and get that cloying sour smell.

Mind you, what about yourself? Surely you could help me with a few of the chores around here. Just a little, not much, but all you do is sit there and stare.

Oh, I am sorry, Alfred. Don't fret so. We'll be fine. As long as that man doesn't poke his nose in. Yes, I know it is my fault. I am sorry, Alfred. Now, how's about breakfast? At least he has delivered the milk and I have some cereal in. That super sweet stuff with chocolate pieces that you like.

Did you see, Alfred? He ran toward me yelling that he needed to see you. Can you imagine it? Oh my goodness, that would never do. You need your rest to recover. Yes, you do. Not to fret. I'll get the breakfast. Do you want a bowl? No? You're sure?

Okay then, Alfred. If you're feeling sick I'll just get myself something.

Have I lost weight? I suppose I have. The body of a girl half my age? I don't think so. A few too many wrinkles for my liking. Do you remember the first time we met? It was summer.

That's right, Alfred, I was wearing blue and it was such a lovely day that I'd gone to walk on the pier. You were so cheeky, walking over and asking me out. I remember blushing and looking at the ground and you did that thing with your hand. You placed it under my chin and brought my eyes to meet yours. I felt like I was looking into your soul and I knew at that moment that we were two that ought to be one. You don't do that any more.

You know, I can forgive you many things, Alfred, but you leaving me is one I'm not sure I can. You are still here, but not.

I don't mind dressing you and looking after you, but if only you would hold me. Sometimes you are so still and quiet I wonder if I am not lying next to a corpse…

I am sorry, Alfred. I think I just lost my mind a little. Not to worry though I can pick up the broken glass. I don't know what came over me. I was running and screaming for no reason. I mean, you are still here. Next to me, where you will always be.

Alfred, there's someone at the door. They're banging on it very loudly. Oh, Alfred, I am so scared. Hold me, please, just until they go away.

"Alex, ram your shoulder into the door."

The large man sighed and placed his frame against the door. It was only a prefab house and never meant to have been permanent housing. He supposed that it was the answer after the war but now they were just rotting eyesores.

The door gave with a splintering crack, more like a gunshot than breaking wood. Mark stepped back and let Alex take the lead. It was his idea after all. Only a few minutes ago they could hear a screaming match going on inside. It had been Alex's idea.

"You seen Alfred lately?" he'd asked.

"No, not for a week or so."

Then the noise started, which is why Mark found himself stepping into the tiny bungalow and looking around, trying to work out what could create that musty smell. Alex had obviously been in the house before because he immediately walked into the room on the right. There was a large window that shed a dirty light.

Mark looked around and wondered why the couple weren't getting more help. They obviously needed it. There was dust and dirt everywhere.

As Alex stepped further into the room something crunched under his foot. They both looked down and could see what appeared to be glass on the floor. A lot of it. Whoever had broken it had really gone to town. It looked like quite a few vases had been hurled to their doom.

"What do you think happened?" Mark asked.

Alex shot him a look that told him to shut up and as he did both men heard a moan. There were two armchairs in the room. One was tipped onto its side but the other was upright and had its back to them. It was an ancient, large wing-backed chair and Mark was certain that was where the moan had come from.

Together they walked forward and peered down at the occupant.

For a moment Mark couldn't understand what he was seeing. It just didn't make sense. Alex went pale and then turned, running from the room, one hand over his mouth. Mark watched and then turned back to the couple.

Alfred was sitting very straight, his head slightly tipped back at just enough angle that Mark could stare into his unseeing and white-blurred eyes.

"Oh my god."

On the lap of the very dead Alfred there was movement and from under the blanket that encircled both of them Missy looked up and into the eyes of the big man.

Oh, I've done it now, Alfred, Missy thought. She had to look away from the horrified eyes of the man. How could he judge? They were soul mates and meant to be together forever. She looked up again but he was gone.

Maybe they'll leave us alone, Alfred, she thought, as she snuggled closer to her husband, not minding that he stole her warmth.

Outside Alex was straightening after throwing up his lunch in the gutter as Mark came stumbling out of the house. He walked to a parked car and placed his hands on the roof, trying to use its solid metal to brace his world.

"Did you see Missy?" Alex asked.

Mark could only nod.

"Was she alive?"

"Almost."

"What do you mean?" Alex said, touching Mark's arm to make him turn to him.

Mark did, but the man who stood there was not the one who had broken the door down. He looked as if his world had been shaken to its roots.

"She was in his lap."

"Dead?" Alex asked, almost hoping that Mark wouldn't answer.

Mark shook his head. "Like a cat. Like the old guy wasn't dead."

"What did she say?"

"Nothing."

Both men turned at the loud thump as the broken door was pushed closed. It wouldn't lock but it still shut. Neither man looked away, transfixed by the mouldering home.

"I'll call…" Alex said.

"Yeah," Mark replied. "She needs help."

17 FOR HER CHILDREN

She sits on the bed waiting. She feels dread but she ought to be grateful. People say they'd do anything for their children, but she really will. He'll come soon, in more ways than one. She smiles ruefully and straightens her lace teddy. The children are at school and as the doorbell rings, she dons her housecoat. She supposes she's lucky, if he could get it anywhere else then he would want rent-money. And money is something she doesn't have. Opening the door he rushes in, undoing his fly as he walks. She closes her eyes thinking of her children.

18 WITHERED BLOOMS

"Mum."

The little girl tugs at her mother's skirt, trying to get her attention.

"Mum."

Still nothing. Her mother continues to talk to Mrs Reynolds from across the road.

"Mum!"

The girl screams and the two adults stop and look at the child standing with them.

"What?" Mum asks.

"She's coming," the little girl whispers, looking at the floor, afraid that she is doing something wrong. Her mother sighs and looks about her. There, a small dot in the distance, someone is walking toward them.

"What's wrong?" Mrs Reynolds says, curious.

Her mother shrugs and then nods at the distant figure. "Bitsie doesn't like the old woman."

Mrs Reynolds turns. "What? Mrs Briggs? She's harmless."

Bitsie buries her head in her mother's coarse woollen skirt. Normally she would never do this as the fabric is scratchy and can make her itch, but she has to do something, the old lady is coming.

Mrs Reynolds tuts. "You don't have to worry, she is harmless."

Bitsie shakes her head and peeks around her mother. "She's odd."

"She has this irrational fear," her mother explains.

"Well, I know Mrs Briggs. She goes to the same church as I do and she is completely harmless."

Mrs Briggs is now close enough to see and Mrs Reynolds raises a hand to her in greeting. She knows that the girl's reaction bothers the old woman. They had been talking about it that Sunday, after service.

"I am worried," Mrs Briggs had said.

"What about?" Mrs Reynolds asked as they cleared away the bibles, placing them back in the locked cupboard. They had been locking it since there had been a break in and someone, probably a teenager, had set light to as many as they could find. The congregation was small and the bibles hadn't been replaced, despite them asking the Priest. He had nodded and reassured them that the powers knew about it. Really, thought Mrs Reynolds, you would have thought the Vatican could afford ten new bibles. So, for the time being, they either bought their own or shared, and locked the last remaining moth-eared black covered books away.

Mrs Briggs was looking at her and for a moment Mrs Reynolds was worried that she had missed something.

"It's the children," Mrs Briggs said.

"What about them?"

"They have started to run away from me."

"Why?"

"I don't know..." Mrs Briggs paused and then looked around. She leant forward and whispered. "They call me a witch."

Mrs Reynolds raised her eyebrows in shock, although the truth was that she already knew. She'd heard them. But she had done nothing. It wasn't her problem. But now, looking at the ancient lady in front of her, she felt shame. "They are only children."

Mrs Briggs gave her a wry smile. "And they can be the cruellest creatures on the earth."

Mrs Reynolds blinked, but before she could answer Father was calling for her. It was in that moment that she looked at the older lady; truly looked at her. What she saw was a bent old woman, world-weary and tired. Her grey hair was clean but thin, showing the pinkness of her scalp. Her eyes were red rimmed and watery, even the colour looked washed out. Surely they had been a vibrant blue, almost violet, but now the light blue orbs swam in red tinged pools with heavy lids. When had Mrs Briggs started to bend over? It must have been gradual as Mrs Reynolds couldn't remember it happening suddenly. It was obvious though that she could no longer straighten. Her clothes were the same she had always worn, but now they looked thinner, and despite it being a beautiful summer day, she had about four layers on. One bobbly jumper on top of another, all of them with the colours washed out.

Mrs Reynolds could see what the children saw and it was an old woman who was so old that she seemed scary, her face distorted by wrinkles that seemed so deep they appeared more like cracks.

As she was staring Mrs Briggs turned and raised an age-spotted hand in farewell. Mrs Reynolds echoed the gesture and watched as she shuffled off. The Priest walked over to her.

"Mrs Reynolds," he said, and she could tell by his tone he was going to ask her something. Normally she would make her escape but this time he was blocking the exit. "Have you noticed that Mrs Briggs seems…"

"Tired," Mrs Reynolds finished for him.

"Yes. I was wondering if you could take over some of her duties."

"Well, Father, I am very busy," she started, looking at her watch.

"True, but I am concerned that we are asking too much of her."

That made Mrs Reynolds pause. "But she only does the flowers."

"Oh no," Father said. "She cleans the church and the vicarage twice a week. She also washes up after the teas and cleans the kitchen."

After every service there was tea and cake, but Mrs Reynolds thought the cleaning up was done by the PTA or someone similar. "She does all that?"

"Yes, and I am worried..."

"How much do you pay her?" Mrs Reynolds interrupted.

"What?" Father seemed taken aback by this. "Nothing. She is a Christian."

Mrs Reynolds pursed her lips together. "I'll take over washing up after the teas on Sunday." She started to push past him and then stopped. "Does she cook for you as well?"

Father blushed and stammered. "Sometimes."

Mrs Reynolds sniffed and walked away. She felt her faith falter and for a moment she felt rage against the man behind her, but then it dissipated. She could have asked, she could have made it easier. Instead she had let it happen, not really asking any questions, just happy she wasn't doing it herself.

Now, standing in the road with one of the children who probably called Mrs Briggs a witch, she felt a need to do something. "You mustn't be afraid of Mrs Briggs. She is a good person and a Catholic."

Both Bitsie and her mother look at her.

"She works for no money for the church…"

Mum interrupts her. "At her age?"

Mrs Reynolds blushes the same way the Priest had done. "Yes. I've started helping though."

"But she smells," Bitsie says.

Mrs Reynolds sighs. "It's the flowers. She changes them in the church and over time the smell seems to have stuck. But she is a wonderful person."

Bitsie looks at her mother's friend and shakes her head. "No, she can't be. If she was then people would be nice to her and talk or help her. But they don't. Instead, they push her out of the way and ignore her."

Mrs Reynold's eyes go wide with shock. "Why you…"

But Mum is already pulling her little girl away. "Bitsie, that doesn't make Mrs Briggs bad. It just shows how others are mean to her."

"Like bullies?" her daughter asks.

"Yes."

Behind them Mrs Reynolds listens as they leave.

Mrs Briggs catches up to her. "Are you alright?" she asks.

"Yes, thank you."

"Can I help you with anything?" Mrs Brigg asks and transfers the weight of the dead flowers onto her other hand. They never used to be this heavy.

"No, I'm fine," Mrs Reynolds says and stalks away, ignoring Mrs Briggs and putting as much distance as she can between herself and the child.

Mrs Briggs turns and is stopped by a small child. The girl holds out her hand and takes the bag of withered blooms. "Mum says you aren't a witch and I've got to help you."

Mrs Briggs watches the child for a moment. The girl looks into the bag.

"That smells bad."

"It does," Mrs Briggs says. "But for a while they were beautiful."

19 A LIVE HAUNTING

She sits on a bench watching the world go by, a world that doesn't see her. A few greying strands of hair have escaped a careless bun and wave in the cool breeze. It is a chilly day in late September but the sky is clear and so very blue. The bench sits atop a hill surrounded by flowers and small inscribed stones, each a shrine to someone's lost love; perhaps a father or missed parent, or, worse, a child. Yet the woman ignores it all and runs her hand along the empty seat beside her. Her gesture is odd and sensual as if stroking a lover and not an object made of wood and iron. Her hand catches on a rough patch and she winces, drawing a breath through her teeth. An inspection shows a small splinter. Placing her palm against her mouth she prizes it out by catching it between her front teeth. She presses her other hand to the wound to stop any bleeding, not that there'd be much; it was only a shallow cut. Still, a drop falls and hits her black skirt, instantly swallowed into the dark fabric.

Unseen and slightly to her left the gardener continues to rake leaves watching the woman. *Odd one,* he thinks, *comes every day and sits in silence.* At first he thought she was a wife or sister but asking around had led him to find out that she was neither. The man on whose bench she sat had died with his wife in a car accident, leaving no family, and although the view was good the gardener didn't think that anyone would want to spend time in a crematorium. Shrugging, he goes back to the leaves, *but then what did he know?*

The woman shifts in her seat and looks at her hand, *no blood, good.* She doesn't see the drop of black on black, but then she doesn't see much. She refuses to acknowledge her unkempt appearance or the rumpled clothes she wears. Nor does she see that the plump figure she used to be so proud of, with all the curves in the right places, has dissolved into a skeletal exaggeration of her internal reality. Instead, inside her head, she starts a barrage against her coming:

So, Grace, what are you doing here?

No answer, but then Grace isn't expecting one as she really isn't sure. She understands that she misses him, but why she comes, day in and day out, is a mystery, even to her. It is more like a calling, an obsession. His face pops into her head; Tobias Evergreen, and for a moment he is so real that she can even taste him, the man she had given her heart to.

It's not going to stop though, Grace, the sensible part of her said, *every day for over a month you've come here. You've lost everything and what is left is slipping through your fingers.* Grace just stares at the view, not showing any sign of emotion, not even blinking. *And that's the trick isn't it, Grace, to appear normal and sane. Except you aren't, are you?*

Again, Grace doesn't answer herself. She doesn't think she needs to. Tobias is all she thinks about. He had been full of charm and bluster. She'd met him in a pub in town, one of those huge chain pubs that had converted the local cinema. She missed the cinema with its old wood doors and sticky carpet. Anyway, she'd gone to see what they'd done to the beloved building and that's where she met him. He'd started a conversation at the bar but it wasn't until their third date that he'd told her about his wife. By then she was caught. *He couldn't leave her,* he'd said, *disabled.* He'd pleaded with her to understand. *She'd be alone if I left,* he wailed. She'd nodded and gently told him she did understand and that she would be there for him, always.

So now she sits on a bench in the cold and can't believe that all those years ago it had just taken one conversation to discard all her convictions. What of her promise never to be the other woman? Why had she so easily forgotten her mother's face and the loud arguments that blighted her childhood? Anger threads its way through her body and takes hold of her heart. Now she knows that the last nine years were a lie, they were wasted, all those days lost. She closes her eyes and forces a sob back into her throat, making her chest ache. She wants to go back, she wants; no, that isn't strong enough, she desires it; no, she deserves and demands it with the very essence of her being.

Why then are you here, wasting time? A small voice asks. *Surely the dead haunt the living? I'm not sure it works this way round...*

No, Grace thinks, *it doesn't work,* but this is as close as she can get to him. Slowly, she turns in her seat and gazes at the shiny plaque. She runs a finger along it, feeling the cold indentations of the brassy words.

Tobias Evergreen and his beloved wife, Karen, taken so suddenly before their time.

Grace doesn't know who drafted the words to this plaque but 'before their time' in her mind was not soon enough. Although she supposes that she could have found out at any point in the last nine years. She could have gone to his home and met the wonderful crippled wife, maybe posing as a fake salesperson or someone doing a survey. Instead she'd buried her head in the sand just like a stupid big bird. She'd never met Karen, never shaken her hand or discussed clothes... Briefly Grace's lip curls back in a sneer. *Crippled. Ha!* Karen hadn't been crippled; she was as able bodied as she was herself. That day of the funeral Grace had arrived in full widow's weeds, even a veil of soft lace that floated around her face. She's sitting at the back, thinking it best to hide; after all you don't want to be recognised as the deceased's mistress.

She'd learnt of Tobias' death from the newspaper, the front cover filled with the picture of the smashed car. The doorman at Tobias's expensive apartment block had told her the time of the funeral and so she went. She'd taken her seat and begun her silent and tear-filled farewell to her soul mate. At first she hadn't taken much notice of the front of the church but slowly, as people appeared to place pictures onto the table in front of the double coffins, closed of course, she'd dried her eyes and tried to clear her vision. From where she sat she could see most of the framed images were of holiday snaps; Tobias and Karen sailing; Tobias and Karen in the Caribbean. At least she assumed it was Karen as she had never seen her before, but the pretty blond matched Tobias' type. She remembered at the time finding it odd that everyone placed photos of Karen before she had become crippled. Except...

Grace had stood and gone up to the photos, ignoring the whispers that her presence caused. There were Tobias and Karen in front of the London Olympic park entrance and there was Tobias sailing in the shirt she had given him, a violent yellow number that was a joke purchase but that he'd cherished. There was Karen, happily smiling, standing straight Karen. Grace had stumbled back to the bench and sat down, keeping her head lowered until everyone turned round. She'd wanted to scream as the hurt and anger had overtaken her. Instead she'd sat through the whole funeral and then left to go home.

Now, sitting on Tobias' bench, she felt the same anger that had flashed through her that day. No, she knew that the shit had just not wanted to leave his lovely wife and why should he when he could get the best of both worlds, a wife to cook and clean, and a whore to massage his cock when he needed it?

A small voice in the back of her head quietly reminds her that she enjoyed their time together as well as him, but Grace pushes it aside. Thanks to him she feels abandoned and abused, alone at forty two and with no prospects. She wishes that she had never met him, that nine years ago she had given him the cold shoulder. But now, she misses him so much it hurts sometimes. No, actually it hurts all the time. Grace knows that she isn't coping without him, but her relationship with Tobias is now one of love and hate. *Can you have a relationship with a ghost?* He had become her life, her means of existence. All she had done every day was make herself more appealing, and she only spent money on him. She had ousted her own disapproving family and her friends had slowly disappeared as her all-consuming passion for Tobias had precluded everything. In the end he had paid for everything. But the family had put a stop to that. Just the other day she'd been told by her landlord that the rental payments appeared to have stopped. *Appeared to have*, what a phrase, how can money appear to have stopped? She had then gone to the bank and been told that not only was there no money going into her account, but it had stopped just after Tobias' death and was she aware that she was a grand in debt? Grace had never been in debt before and her future included a seedy apartment and having to sell her clothes just to eat. Of course she had no appetite, so at least those bills were small. Now she spends all her time sitting on the bench his ashes are scattered around, just to get close to him.

Heaving herself up she pats the bench like a friend and walks away wearing her self-loathing like a heavy cloak.

The gardener watches her leave and shakes his head, he knows the type. She would be back tomorrow. He'd seen it before. She would pine until there was nothing left; until she was like the ghosts she desired to meet. Then he supposed he would have to dig another hole and place another plaque. One thing you could count on was death, but he never understood why some people insisted on running toward it.

PHILIA

friendship

20 LIFE'S MYSTERY

He was coming towards me in the car park as I was leaving. I stopped and wound the window down. He looked his age today though I didn't know exactly what that was, except as soon as he began to speak a mischievous twinkle appeared in his eye and he lost years.

I said, "Mike. Are you ok?"

"Remember the Canadian girl I told you about," he said.

"The one you knew when she was twelve?"

"Yes, seventeen now. You know we had all that stuff with her mother. She's coming over in July. We're going to bring her down to The Harbourmaster. I'll give you a shout. You can see what all the fuss was about."

I nodded and walked over to my pick-up. Could I even remember what the fuss was about? Vaguely I remembered the girl, but not the problem. All that came into my head was a child, too skinny in jeans and an old frayed t-shirt looking at me with such huge eyes I thought at the time I would swing at Mike for hurting her. There you go. I knew that as soon as I thought around it I would remember something.

The mother had been doing some exchange course with Lampeter Uni. I couldn't remember what, but she had been renting a room just on the outskirts, a pink farmhouse. I grin, remembering the parties and the friends. Strange how in just five years everything can change. Back then I'd been a trainee central heating fitter, now I worked as a farm labourer. Well, no one was expecting the bottom to fall out of the market. Still, those days had been great, although the business with Tracey had been a little edgy. This girl had run in from the farmhouse and said someone was beating on her mum. So I'd roused myself, trying to shake off the effects of the weed and gone in the house. I'd told the kid to wait outside. She didn't though. It was just as if I'd acquired a small living shadow, so I just ignored her.

The mother's room had been at the top of the stairs and, as I walked up, I heard the noises. Her Mum wasn't being hurt, in fact she sounded like she was enjoying it, but the child had prodded me, eyes full of tears and bottom lip quivering, and I'd thought I'd have to do something. I mean this ought not be her first experience of sex. She thought her mum was being hurt. So I banged on the door and yelled that he was to stop, that I had the girl out here and she thought her mum was in pain.

There was silence for a moment and then the door opened a crack. There was Mike. I was shocked. I mean the kid's mum must have been about twenty eight but Mike was in his fifties. He had looked at me and I'd moved slightly to show the kid. He'd nodded and went back inside. I could hear hushed voices and then a woman appeared. I recognised her as the girl's mum. Anyhow, this kid hurled herself into her mum's arms and I'd just given a little wave and left.

Back outside I'd settled myself next to the fire and smoked a little. I was just starting to drop off again when the kid appeared.

"Uncle Mike says I am to stay with you while he and Mum play tickle."

Play tickle! I had looked at her. "How old are you?"

The kid had smiled and I saw in that smile a child too old for her years. This kid would one day become a beautiful woman. "I know." She had slouched into a sitting position next to me. "They are having sex."

I grunted a reply, suddenly very hot. What the hell was I gonna say if the kid wanted me to explain.

She turned her big brown eyes to me, saw me all hot and bothered and laughed. "Don't worry, I know all about sex." That laugh! I mean, she was a child, but that laugh was a woman's.

"If you knew, why'd you come and get me?"

The kid shrugged. "I get pissed."

I just stayed silent. She reached for my spliff and I moved it out of her way. "Not on my watch."

She'd pulled this face then and she had looked younger than twelve. "She never spends time with me, just with her boys."

"Her boys?"

The kid nodded and tried again for the weed. "Please," she whined.

"No chance. It'll kill your intelligence."

"What about you?" She said, pouting.

I grinned. "Planning on fitting radiators. Don't need brains for that."

The kid had given this cruel smile, almost a sneer. "No, you don't." She sat for a minute in silence, listening to the distant traffic and the noise of the rural night. A tawny owl was hunting and I was about to point out which noise it was making when the kid looked at me.

"She has lots of blokes."

The look she gave me was so sad. I leaned across and pulled her into a hug, the kind I give my big sister. She stiffened and then relaxed. Then I told her about the sounds and pointed out the different animals. I told her the name of the stars and how they changed throughout the year. We talked and laughed and for a moment the kid had forgotten her mum and what was going on upstairs. Hell, I enjoyed myself. It reminded me of the times I used to go camping as a child and my dad had pointed out the stars and wildlife to me. Not that I thought of myself as her dad. I was only eighteen at the time. At some point she asked where I lived and I told her.

Then Mike was there saying he needed a lift and I said I'd give him one. I hugged the girl and left. It was five days later that she turned up crying. Her mum had told her to get lost so she could spend time with Mike. Right there on my doorstep I wanted to hurt Mike for causing those tears. Instead I asked if she had eaten. She said no, so I took her to the local greasy spoon and watched as she devoured a mountain of food. She said they were leaving in a couple of days and I suddenly felt quite sad.

That sadness had stayed with me for a while. Yet, as I started the pick-up in that car park I knew that I would go and see her at the Harbourmaster. Mike was about to leave and I pulled alongside. "Did she ask to see me?"

"Who?" Mike said, looking cagey

"Tracey."

Mike frowned and then smiled. "She did. Odd thing that, I don't remember you meeting her."

"I knew her," I said softly and sit back wondering.

Mike shrugged and put his foot on the gas. "Told me to say to you that she remembers the food and would like to repay the kindness." He sniffed in the direction he was going to go. "Shame though."

"What?"

"She's already engaged. Still, what do you expect with her

mother."

And then he was gone. I sat for a moment watching his retreating car. I remembered that kid and I wondered. She had said she wanted to work with wildlife. I had a feeling though that she wasn't going to make it. Hell, that time I had with her had made me change my apprenticeship. Now I was doing what I loved, farming, but most of my friends thought me daft to give up money for happiness. Still, I thought, as I pulled out, I wouldn't change it for anything. Maybe I'd harboured a dream that she would turn out to not follow her mum's footsteps, but perhaps that was too big an ask. At least she remembered me.

Driving off I decided to go to the pub when Mike called, if Mike called. I was curious to find out what had happened to that big eyed child in her too big clothes.

21 THE PRICE OF FRIENDSHIP

"Hey, Rachel!"

Turning, I wave at Dawn. She's looking good. Wish I could say the same about myself. Recovering from the flu has left me drained and feeling a little tired. I just hope she wants to talk to me and not just pump me for information and gossip. Don't get me wrong I do like Dawn but she is an incredible talker. With her around you have no secrets. Once you tell her everyone knows.

"Hi, Dawn."

"Come on. I got us a table over here."

I sit, glad she's chosen a nice place. There are few things I hate but bad tea is one of them. Here it won't be a mug and an insipid teabag floating in the top. Instead, I'll get a little teapot and milk jug. The only drawback is the cup. One day I will find the perfect place which does everything and lets you have a mug. I knowingly admit I am a tea snob.

"I've already ordered. I got you a tea," Dawn informed me.

"Thanks." Now I'm perturbed. What is going on? Dawn never pays for anything.

"How are you doing?" She asks and puts a comforting hand on my arm.

"Fine," I say slowly. "Getting over the flu but apart from that I'm okay."

"Good." She smiles a sad smile. "How is Charlie?"

This throws me. Charlie is a friend who just moved away. Could Dawn be concerned about that? "She's fine. Settled in all right."

"Is she getting on with her partner?" This makes me grin. Charlie is now living with Tasha and they are actually engaged. Of course Dawn has an issue with Charlie's sexual preference so will only refer to Tasha as the partner.

"They are getting along great. In fact she just got engaged."

"Oh no! I'm so sorry, Rachel. If there's anything I can do please let me know. Even if you want to go into one of those bars." Dawn is now patting my hand and giving me a pitying smile.

Carefully I remove my hand. "Why would I be upset?"

"Well, losing your girlfriend."

I blink. My girlfriend? "I don't have a girlfriend."

"I know," she says with that pitying look agian. "Not now she's moved in with Tasha."

"Moved in...," I repeat. "You think I was going out with Charlie?"

"Well, yes. You were."

"Er, no. We're just friends."

Dawn blinks at me. "It's nothing to be ashamed of."

"I know it isn't," I say, leaning forward. "But I'm not a lesbian and I've never been out with Charlie in that sense."

"But," she stammered, "you go to dinner...."

"We both like to try new restaurants."

"... And the movies."

"We both like movies. We are just friends."

"But I told...." She falls silent and looks at her watch. "Goodness, is that the time? I must be going!"

And that was it. I sat. I paid the bill and I fumed. This was the reason why I hadn't had many boyfriends, or a least, local boyfriends. Getting back home I picked up the phone and dialled Charlie's number from memory. Tash picked up. "Hey, put me on speaker. You aren't going to believe what I've just found out…."

22 FLOOD

Rain water is so very different from snow. When it snows so hard that we are marooned in the house we are alone. We sit in front of a fire and warm our hands, cooking from the stock cupboard and waiting for the snow plough. But the rain is so very different. Too much snow and you are transported to Lapland and Christmas, no matter what the time of year. In a way snow is comforting; it allows you to wear the thickest jumper and explore the surroundings of your back garden as if it is virgin land and you an intrepid explorer. True, it becomes wearing and you can long for spring, but you are always able to go somewhere dry and warm. With the rain everything becomes damp, even the air. In Wales, where I live, we have what is called a soft day. This is when the rain falls as if it were relaxed and really not bothered about hitting the ground. You can see tourists around Aberaeron suddenly turn up their collars and shiver in their plastic macs. The locals will smile and nod and not make any difference to their clothing at all. We know, you see, that a soft day will always become a bright day, that the clouds will part and the sun will beat down with a vengeance.

On this soft day, I woke as normal. I live alone and have only a ginger tom cat for company. And I can make my life as I see fit. I have family but they live far and wide, from Australia, to the Netherlands and London. I see some quite regularly, but I was in a dry spell as far as visits were concerned. Not that I minded; the kids have their own lives. Until that summer I'd lived a fairly quiet life. True, if I went into town people would stop and say hi, and I would never have a trip without someone stopping me for a chat. So, I was happy in my solitude. I'm not a people person, or at least I didn't think I was.

The rain had been falling since early that morning, just like a soft day and I was expecting it to clear. It didn't. Instead, it came down harder. It went from a relaxed fall to an insistent pounding. I thought nothing of it. The road is directly in front of the property, but I'm in a little dip, like the other five houses in the row of terraces, but I just ignored the sound. There was no wind, and I looked out. The words that came to me were that the sky was falling. It truly looked like that, as if the clouds were too heavy and were dragging down the atmosphere. I didn't go out so I don't know whether the rain was cold or warm, not then at least.

It rained all morning and afternoon and as the sky turned dark it seemed to get even heavier. I wasn't scared. Why would I be? I did notice a smell, like a sewery damp smell. It was faint and I remember going to the bathroom, but the toilet was fine and seemed to be working well. The smell was worse in the kitchen and I remember that I thought the sink was blocked. Foolish, I know. If I'd gone out the back I might have noticed there was a problem.

You see, all of the terraces have their own independent septic tanks, onions. They look like the vegetable they are named after and are sunk into the ground with a soakaway to catch the run off. The onion in my back garden is below the house and the soakaway below that. If I'd put my head out of the door and had a look I'd have seen that the soakaway was under water and the onion was about to go the same way. The smell was the effluent rising and making its way toward the house. I didn't though. Instead I poured some bleach down the sink. I know it's bad for the tank but sometimes it's all that will help. Then I put the kettle on.

I was just making tea when the knocking came. Oddly, it was from the back door and I walked over and looked out of the window. It's one of those doors with a solid bottom and glass top. I couldn't see anything, but I did notice that the wind had picked up. It wasn't violent but I remember thinking that it was enough to bang my wind chimes against the wall. Perhaps this was naive and, looking back, the wind just wasn't strong enough, but I am a pragmatist and will always look for a logical explanation. That appeared logical.

I made my tea and took it to the small table in the kitchen. I live in the kitchen. I do use the living room at night but during the day I can be found at that table writing or making some craft or other. I also bake. I am quite a hand at producing small things, like tiny bara briths and small sponge cakes. The kitchen is the heart of the home, and that was where I was sitting as the water came in.

When you see the floods on the TV, those big panoramas of fields flooded, the water seems to move slowly, but this did not. The water was fast and violent. It did give me warning; a drip, drip from the bottom of the door. I heard it and looked up, deciding it must be the tap, ever logical. Then the lower panel in the door just disappeared. Later, the neighbour said he found it in the living room, but at the time it just appeared to vanish. The water shot inside and hit the chair I was sitting on, which immediately tilted over and I was in the water. It was so cold, mind-numbingly cold, and I froze, despite being completely submerged. It was my need to breathe that got me moving. I pushed with my legs and my head popped up.

I wasn't in the kitchen though. I was in the hall and heading toward the front door at a frightening speed. I put up my hands to break my head-long journey and found I was still clutching my cup. I dropped it. I tried to get my feet under me. I'd worked out I was only in about three feet of water, but I couldn't stand. Every time I put my feet down or tried to stop I was swept back. I was spinning in the water. I hit the front door with my back and it was hard. It knocked the wind out of me, but did allow me to see what was coming. In front of me and bearing down was the table and chair I'd recently been sitting at. Bracing my back I managed to get to my feet but I couldn't push against the water. I was screaming and I could hear people outside. The only problem was it was tourist season, and during that time I lock the door. I felt the handle go. I looked to where the key hung but there was just an empty hook. The water had claimed it.

Before me the stairs rose like some safe haven. If I got there then I could go upstairs. The water wasn't upstairs. I think I was in shock, but I gathered all the strength I had and pushed away from the door and toward that beautiful carpet mountain.

I didn't make it, but I was able to avoid the initial collision with the table. The only problem was that all my furniture was being swept to the front door. I tried desperately to keep my feet, but I got caught up with one of the dining room chairs and I went under. Oddly, the fear I had felt before had relaxed into numbness. It might have been shock or the cold. I was accepting my fate. They say sound carries much better underwater which, I suppose, was why I heard the people outside; my neighbours.

"We have to get the door open," one was yelling.

"I'll get an axe," another said and then I heard a voice I recognised, young Mrs Black. "I have a key," she yelled.

I was starting to feel fuzzy around the edges and at some point I'd closed my eyes, because I could see no light. I think I may have been dying. Then I was moving forward, fast.

They had opened the door and I had flowed out. The water was lower than in my house and the pressure had carried me past my rescuers and into the road, although the road was under water.

I felt myself lifted and I remember thinking I was alive, after all. Why would I feel, if I wasn't? Mary said, "Is she still breathing?"

And someone else answered, "no."

I felt myself being lifted and placed on my back. Then someone leaned over and I felt a kiss, except instead of tenderness I felt my chest move and my lungs fill. Then my senses exploded as I coughed and began to breathe on my own. The first thing I felt was pain. Many years ago my mother had once said that pain reminds you that you are alive, and as it blossomed in my chest and poured throughout my body I welcomed it.

"Mrs Mills?" I heard a voice say and I opened my eyes. I was looking at the handsome face of my neighbour. Paul, I thought his name was. Lived with a young pregnant wife.

"Daisy," I rasped, my throat hurting, "call me Daisy."

Paul smiled and he helped me sit up. I looked around. I was lying on damp ground just up from the houses. All the homes were flooded. "Did we all get out?" I whispered.

"Yes, Daisy, we all did."

After that our little gang of flood refugees stuck together. When we were finally able to move back six months later, my life was changed. We talk over the fence and get together for barbeques, when the Welsh weather allows. I laugh more and, although still solitary, my life is surrounded by family, my flood family.

Kate Murray

ABOUT THE AUTHOR

Kate Murray has been only writing since 2010 when her Aunt brought her a leather bound journal for Christmas. Nothing unusual about that, but she didn't write, in fact she'd only tried to keep a diary for one year. She had done it but it had been a chore. So she started 2011 by enrolling on to a local writing course. It was free and she thought why not, after all she was always telling people stories. That's where she differs, you see she is dyslexic and has been actively steered away from writing. Don't get me wrong, her parents are really supportive and now she's at university studying an MA in creative writing she has a mass of support. But that first step into the writing group was terrifying. She's now studying at the University of Wales, Trinity Saint David and thoroughly enjoying it.

This is Kate's second short story anthology; the first came out in January 2014 and is called 'The Phantom Horse'.

Raging Aardvark Publishing

Champion of the short story and its derivatives, Raging Aardvark Publishing aims to provide space for emerging writers to demonstrate their talents to a wider community.

Totally passionate about the short story form and ways to support the creative process; it's our goal to foster positive growth within the international writers community for these authors.

http://ragingaardvark.com

www.ingramcontent.com/pod-product-compliance
Lightning Source LLC
Chambersburg PA
CBHW060938120626
46557CB00003B/1051